Note to Readers

While the Schmidt and Allerton families are fictional, the events they find themselves in actually happened. During 1916 and 1917, while Europe was being torn apart by one of the bloodiest wars in history, people in the United States couldn't agree about whether or not to join the conflict.

Feelings against Germany grew more hostile as German U-boats continued to blow merchant vessels out of the water, killing many of the people onboard. The German government claimed U.S. ships were carrying war supplies to England, but the U.S. government said the ships were only being used for civilian supplies.

Many American young men, tired of waiting for the U.S. to declare war, joined the American Field Ambulance and other volunteer groups that supported the war effort in Europe. Finally in the spring of 1917, the U.S. declared war on Germany. As the country organized its factories and young men for the war effort, German Americans became the targets of anger and discrimination.

PRELUDE
to
WAR

Norma Jean Lutz

PUBLISHING, INC.
Uhrichsville, Ohio

To the Tulsa Christian Writers Club:
An oasis and feeding ground for hungry, searching writers.

© MCMXCVIII by Barbour Publishing, Inc.

ISBN 1-57748-410-X

Published by Barbour Publishing, Inc.
P.O. Box 719
Uhrichsville, Ohio 44683
http://www.barbourbooks.com

 Member of the
Evangelical Christian
Publishers Association

Printed in the United States of America.

Cover illustration by Peter Pagano.
Inside illustrations by Adam Wallenta.

CHAPTER 1
Mother's Helper

Edie watched as Aunt Frances pulled on her rose-colored kid gloves. Three-year-old Harry was tugging at his mother's skirts and dragging a bedraggled brown teddy bear behind him. The bear had one eye missing and a little hole in the back where the stuffing peeked out.

"Me go, Mama," he said with a whimper. "Me go, too."

"Not this time, Harry." Aunt Frances leaned down to pat his head. "Cousin Edith is going to look after you this afternoon."

Edie stepped forward to reach for Harry. "We'll have a good time together," she said. But he swung a balled-up fist.

"No. Don't want Edie." He puckered his face, ready for a cry.

Aunt Frances just smiled. In a softer voice she said, "He'll be fine five minutes after I leave. You know he will."

Edie hoped her aunt was right. The older cousins, Larry and Gloria, were upstairs in the playroom quietly playing with their toys. They wouldn't be as much trouble as Harry.

Edie knelt down to put herself face to face with Harry. This was to be her first time to be a mother's helper for Aunt Frances, her first opportunity to earn money, and she wasn't going to let Harry ruin it. "We'll play horsey in the backyard. Want to play horsey on Edie's back?"

This time he swung the soft teddy at her. "No! Want Mama."

"A c-o-o-k-i-e will work later." Aunt Frances spelled out the magic word. "But be sure to put him up in his high chair so the crumbs aren't scattered all over the house."

Edie nodded. Aunt Frances's house was always spotless. How she did it was a mystery to Edie. The cook, Dory, helped some, but Aunt Frances was the one who attacked dirt with a vengeance. She moved toward the front hallway and stopped at the gilt-framed mirror to straighten her hat, which was dripping with ribbons, feathers, and silk rosettes. Edie not only adored her aunt, she adored the fine clothes she wore as well.

As the wife of a prominent doctor, Frances Allerton felt it was her duty to be properly attired. However, that didn't mean that Edie's aunt was stuffy. Quite the opposite. Aunt Frances was lighthearted and full of fun.

On this particular Saturday afternoon, she was leaving to attend a meeting of the Minneapolis Women's Suffrage Association, of which she was an active member. Dory had the afternoon off. When the idea of Edie becoming a mother's helper first came up, Aunt Frances suggested they begin with "just a few hours." That comment gave Edie to know she was on trial. If this afternoon didn't work out, she might not have a second chance.

Edie's older brothers, Tim and Carl, both had jobs and were able to help with the family income. Her older sister, Lydia, worked after school and on Saturdays in the basement at Woolworth's. Even Mama was employed as a typist at the Wynlan Freight Company. So with Papa working as a foreman at the Northwest Consolidated Flour Mill, everyone was employed but Edie. Now was her big opportunity.

From the hall table, Aunt Frances picked up her traveling desk, covered in green morocco. She lifted the lid to see that her notes, pens, and papers were all in place. Nodding slightly, she closed it again. Aunt Frances served as the recording secretary for her local organization, which meant she was continually keeping records and tending to reams of correspondence.

Edie watched her aunt's every move. When she grew up, she wanted to be just like Aunt Frances. But since she was only eleven-and-a-half, becoming a grown-up seemed eons away.

Just as Aunt Frances pulled her parasol from the umbrella stand, a purring motor sounded out front.

"There's my ride." Aunt Frances stopped at the front door and turned to Edie. "Now don't worry. You'll do fine. I'm pleased that you want to help me out."

"Me go!" Harry said. He stood there rubbing his eyes with his fist as though to push back the tears.

"Not this time, precious. Mama will be back soon."

Edie reached down to pick up the chunky boy and perch him on her hip. The little guy was built like a rock. Thankfully he didn't swing a fist at her this time.

The door was open now, and Edie could see the Rio touring

car parked elegantly at the curb. Inside were three other ladies, adorned in frocks as fine as Aunt Frances's and finer.

"I'll be back about three," she said. "I've left the telephone number where I can be reached on the desk in my study. Bye now."

"Bye," Edie called back. "Wave bye to Mama," Edie said to Harry.

"Me go!" With that, he reached with both arms high in the air and made a backward lunge, almost causing Edie to lose her grasp. She clutched him more tightly and didn't let go of him to wave to Aunt Frances.

She closed the door as the car pulled away, and Harry burst into tears. "Mama! Want Mama," he wailed. His feet beat a tattoo on her hips and the teddy thudded against her back.

"I know where there's a cookie," she said in a singsong voice. "But I don't think you know." Twirling him around she sang, "A cookie, a cookie. Can you find a cookie?"

The flow of tears dissipated to a slow leak. "Tookie jar," he mumbled around his first finger, which was now jammed into his mouth.

"Is the cookie in the icebox?"

Harry vigorously shook his head. A little smile appeared. "Tookie jar," he repeated.

"Under the table?" They were in the kitchen now. After setting him down, Edie ceremoniously peered beneath the tablecloth on the kitchen table.

Harry gave a little giggle. "No," he said and vigorously shook his head, making his curls bounce. Pointing a stubby finger at the cabinet, he said, "Tookie jar." Now he was bouncing on his toes.

"Well, well. Let's just see." She took down the fat stoneware jar and lifted the lid. The aroma of sugar cookies wafted out.

The jar was nearly full.

"Tookie, tookie," Harry squealed.

"Into the high chair first." Edie lifted the hinged tray on the wooden high chair, letting it rest behind the chair. She reached down to heave the toddler up into the chair and replaced the tray. From the cabinet drawer, she took out one of Aunt Frances's linen tea towels and used it to tie around Harry's tummy, just as she'd seen Aunt Frances do on numerous occasions. That would keep him from climbing out.

Slapping his hands on the tray with loud smacking noises, he cried, "Tookie, tookie!"

"Be patient, Harry. I'm moving as fast as I can."

As she handed him a golden cookie topped with colored sprinkles and replaced the stoneware lid, a crash sounded from upstairs followed by a cry that would wake the dead.

Edie pushed the cookie jar to the back of the cabinet and ran to the stairway. "What's going on up there?" she asked as she hurried up the stairs.

Pushing into the playroom, she saw Gloria sitting on the floor sobbing. Her doll dishes were scattered in disarray on the floor near her doll table. Pointing to Larry, she said, "He did it. He spoiled my tea party."

"She messed up my airplanes," he countered, pointing to his collection of toy airplanes in a jumble on the floor.

"Not on purpose," she whimpered with a sniff. "I accidentally stumbled over them."

"Was too on purpose." He picked up one that was a miniature biplane. "This one's wing is bent, and it's my favorite."

Edie pursed her lips in disgust. These two had more toys than three families of children, and here they were fighting over them.

"Now stop arguing, both of you," Edie commanded.

9

Larry, at age eight, was nearly as big as Edie and was not in favor of having her take care of him. When he first learned Edie was going to be their caretaker for the afternoon, he announced so all could hear, "I don't need anyone to watch out for me. I'm big enough to watch out for myself."

Edie pulled a hankie from the pocket of her pinafore and proceeded to mop Gloria's tears. "It doesn't matter if it was on purpose or an accident, the point is to forgive and forget. Now Gloria, you tell Larry you're sorry and help him straighten his airplane formation. Larry, you tell Gloria you're sorry and help fix her tea table."

"Tea tables are for girls," he retorted.

"I'm not asking you to play; I'm asking you to pick them up. I'd hate to have to become a tattletale, but I'm going to have to report to your mother everything that went on in her absence."

"I don't want Gloria's old help with my airplanes," Larry said.

Gloria pushed her jet black ringlets away from her face, her eyes flashing. "Well, I don't want you even touching my doll dishes."

Edie heaved a sigh. "Just so you get them picked up and stop fussing." As she turned to leave the playroom, the knocker sounded on the front door. "Oh now what?" Tripping down the steps, she hollered back at them, "I'll be back in a minute to check to see that you did what I told you."

Edie pulled open the front door to see her best friend, Janelle Swearingen. "Nell, am I glad to see you." She reached out to grab her friend's arm and pulled her inside. "This job isn't as easy as it might seem."

Janelle lived only a few blocks from Aunt Frances, and the two girls played together whenever Edie was there visiting—

which was quite often. Nell smiled and said, "I thought you might need some company."

"Company? I need a hand. I'm busy with Larry and Gloria upstairs. They just had a real tussle. Harry's in the kitchen eating a cookie. Would you be a dear and go check on him?"

"What're friends for?" Nell rushed off down the hall while Edie hurried back upstairs to find the two children still had not done what she told them.

"He won't say he's sorry," Gloria said with a little whine in her voice.

Larry's smile was a smirk. "I've always been taught to let ladies go first."

"This is silliness!" Edie said, nearly ready to lose her patience.

"Edie!" came Nell's call from the foot of the stairs. "I think you'd better come down here."

"What is it?"

"Come and see!"

"You two apologize right now, even if you have to say it in unison. Get this place straightened up, and then you can each have a cookie."

Not waiting to see if they obeyed, she rushed down the stairs, her heart pounding.

Nell had already hurried back to the kitchen. When Edie pushed through the swinging door, the first thing she saw was an empty high chair with a limp tea towel hanging down one side. A kitchen chair had been pushed to the cabinet, the cookie jar was on its side, and broken and crumbled sugar cookies were scattered on the cabinet and floor.

"Harry! Where's Harry?"

Nell, her brown doelike eyes wide, stood in the middle of the room and pointed to the pantry.

Edie moved slowly toward the pantry and peeked behind the door. "Oh, my!"

Harry sat on the floor with the bucket of sorghum molasses open. Molasses was all over him, and he was dipping out another fistful as she entered.

Looking up at her, he shot her a wide grin. "Mm, good," he said.

CHAPTER 2
Best Friends

Edie was sure she was going to faint. She clutched the pantry door frame. "Harry Edwin Allerton. You've just cost me my first real job."

At that moment, Larry came downstairs and peeked around to see what was going on. "Doesn't look to me like you're going to be a very good mother's helper," he stated dryly.

"I might have been if you two hadn't been fussing upstairs like two little imps." Tears burned Edie's eyes, and she blinked hard.

"Nobody said you had to come up and start bossing us around."

"Don't say that, Larry." Gloria came up behind her older brother, pushed past him, and put her arms around Edie. With tears in her eyes, she said, "I'm sorry, Edie. I'm sorry we caused you problems."

Edie patted her six-year-old cousin gently. She took a deep breath. No sense in being upset, she told herself. That wouldn't solve anything. "I accept your apology, Gloria. Now let's all work to get this mess cleaned up."

"I'll put water on to heat," Nell said. She found a kettle in the cabinet and filled it at the sink.

"Thanks, Nell. You're such a good friend. Larry, you and Gloria begin picking up the cookies," Edie said.

"I didn't make the mess, and I don't have to clean it up," Larry announced, turning to leave. "I'm going outside to play."

Edie wanted to stop him, but she wasn't sure how. Nor was she sure she needed to. They could get it done without him. She knelt down to take the molasses bucket from Harry. As she did, he reached out to pat her arm with his sticky hand.

"Edie," he said. "Wuv Edie."

"Ugh," she muttered. How Edie hated getting messy and dirty. She'd probably never make a very good mother.

Within the hour, the girls had mopped up the mess in the pantry, Harry was scrubbed and put into a clean romper suit, and the kitchen floor was swept clean of all the broken cookies. Just as Edie felt things were pretty well under control, Larry came running in all out of breath.

"Tabby's having her kittens! Right now. Out there in the shed. Come on." He spun around and raced down the hall toward the back door.

14

"Gracious," Edie said. "What next? I don't know anything about cats having kittens."

Nell gave her a reassuring smile. "There's nothing to know. They do it all themselves." She grabbed Gloria's hand. "Let's go watch."

Edie picked up Harry, slung him on her hip, and followed. The storage shed was at the back of the Allertons' property where their yard bordered that of Mr. and Mrs. Benecroft. The Benecrofts grew a large garden and kept chickens. As they approached the shed, Harry pointed at the chickens. "Chickies," he said.

"He likes the chickens," Gloria told them. "He stuck his finger through the fence once and got pecked, but he's still not afraid of them."

"That's our Harry," Edie said laughing. This boy wasn't afraid of anything.

Nell was right about the kittens. There was nothing to do. The children watched in silence as the mama cat cleaned each tiny baby as it emerged into the world. Edie was fascinated with the miracle unfolding before their eyes. The tabby cat, which had been a stray two years ago, was a much-loved family pet. She didn't seem to mind that her babies were being fussed over almost as soon as they were dry. Their tiny mews filled the air as they tumbled over one another to find places to feed.

And that's where Aunt Frances found them when she came home. She seemed pleased about the kittens' arrival. "Baby kittens are always so much fun," she said. Scooping Harry up in her arms, she motioned for Edie to follow her into the house.

Aunt Frances commended Edie on a job well done and handed her a shiny dime. A whole dime. Edie squeezed it in her hand and then slipped it into the pocket of her pinafore. At first she thought she needn't say anything about the mishaps. But then she thought of what Mama would tell her if she were there. "Honesty's the best policy," she'd say.

"I didn't really do all that good of a job," Edie said, wondering if Aunt Frances might ask for the dime back. Stammering a bit, she did her best to explain what happened without making things look bad for Larry and Gloria.

Aunt Frances's pretty arched brows went up as she listened. When Edie finished, she said, "This is the best way to learn, Edie. I told you Harry was a handful, and now you understand what I mean. It's best never to let him out of your sight."

"Yes, ma'am. I sure learned that all right." Inwardly she cringed, because she'd known that fact already. She shouldn't have left Harry sitting in the kitchen alone. Her older sister, Lydia, would never have done such a silly thing. Lydia was such a take-charge, capable person.

"I commend you on the hard work you did to clean it all up." Aunt Frances put Harry back into his high chair and tied the tea towel around him. "It'll get easier each time. Now you can go play until it's time to take the trolley home."

"Yes, ma'am."

Now that her work was over, Edie and Nell had a couple hours to themselves. They sat on the grass and pronounced spelling words out of Nell's spelling book. The spring spelling bee was coming up, and both girls hoped to win. The April sunshine felt glorious. It was the kind of soft warm day that Edie never wanted to end. She always enjoyed the time she spent with Nell.

Nell didn't have a big family like Edie's. Her older brother Devlin attended school back East, and she seldom got to see

16

him. She'd told Edie many times how lonely she'd been before they met. "You're like the sister I never had," she'd say.

Later, Edie and Nell sat in the glider on the Allertons' front porch, watching the sun sink past the tops of the shade trees and working on their tatting. Aunt Frances had taught them the basic stitches, and now both girls were nearly finished with their first pieces.

The delicate precise loops and stitches fascinated Edie, and she loved watching her coverlet growing inch by inch.

They'd sat quietly working for a time when Edie looked over at Nell and said, "A penny for your thoughts."

Nell stopped working for a moment and gave a big sigh. "I was thinking how easy it is on a lovely day like this to forget there's an awful killing war going on over across the ocean."

"It's not quite so easy for me to forget. Carl brings home the paper almost every day and spouts the headlines as though he were hawking papers on a street corner."

Nell smiled. "Carl's so quiet, I can't imagine him talking that much."

"He talks at home, just not in front of other people."

Nell was quiet again. The glider squeaked as they swung back and forth. Somewhere down the street a dog barked, and the Benecrofts' chickens made lazy clucking noises.

Another reason Edie couldn't forget about the war was because her name was Schmidt. Ever since Germany had invaded Belgium two years ago, then pressed on to attack France, every German American in the country was suspected of terrible things—such as spying and sabotage.

Nell spoke again, breaking the quiet. "Papa says our country may go to war against Germany."

Edie nodded. "My papa says he prays we won't. So many will die if our country is dragged in."

"But if we do. . ." Nell reached out to take Edie's hand.

Edie looked over at her friend, whose hazel eyes were glistening. Was Nell about to cry?

"If we do," Nell began again, "we'll always be friends. No matter what."

Edie didn't have to ask her what she meant. "Thanks, Nell. I agree. We'll always be friends."

At that moment, Aunt Frances came to the front door. "Janelle, your mama telephoned. She says it's time to come home."

Edie jumped up. "Goodness, I'd best get home as well. I've got to get supper on for the family."

The two girls gave one another a hug before parting. On the trolley ride home, Edie thought about what Nell had said about being friends. Some of the kids at school called her a dirty Hun or a dumb Kraut just because she had a German name. But Nell would never do such a thing. Edie thanked God every day for her friendship with Nell.

CHAPTER 3

War News

Truman Vaught was at the house when Edie arrived home. His hat and jacket were hanging in the kitchen. Looking out the kitchen window, she could tell Truman and Carl were busy in Carl's photography darkroom—a converted shed. Eighteen-year-old Truman was a tall gangly young man who worked at the Minneapolis *Tribune*, hence he knew a great deal about cameras and photography. Truman had quit school in eighth grade and begun working to support his widowed mother.

Ever since Carl had traded a few marbles for his first camera, he'd been consumed with a passion for photography. Lydia once said that Carl used his darkroom as a place to hide, but Edie didn't think that was true. Perhaps Lydia didn't understand that Carl liked to be quiet a lot and think.

As Edie peeled potatoes, she noticed Mrs. Bierschwale next door working in her vegetable garden. Twice her husband's leather goods shop had been doused with yellow paint for no other reason than that he was a German American. Edie felt saddened as she watched the bent-over woman. This strange turn of events had aged their neighbor considerably.

By the time Mama and Lydia came home from work, Edie had supper nearly ready. She was just taking the biscuits from the oven when they came breezing in, chattering like two magpies. Lydia was never without something to say.

Mama swooped in to hug Edie and give her a kiss, complimenting her on fixing such a fine meal, then removed her hat and coat and hung them by the back door. Lydia stood by the door with her hands behind her back and a smile on her face.

Edie dumped the baking tin full of biscuits into a large bowl and covered them with a tea towel. "What is it, Lydia?" she asked. "What are you holding?"

"Something special. Something special for the best little cook in all of Minneapolis."

Edie blushed. "Not quite."

"Almost the best?" Lydia said in a teasing tone.

"Close enough to suit me," Mama put in. She pulled her print apron on over her white shirtwaist and long black skirt and took over at the big cookstove.

Putting the biscuits on the table, Edie turned her full attention to her older sister. Lydia used to be such a tomboy, but now, after almost a full term of high school, she'd left all that behind. Edie thought her sister quite attractive now that she styled her hair and wore dresses that flattered her tiny waist. "It must be something from the store," Edie said, her curiosity now thoroughly piqued.

"You're right!" From behind her back Lydia presented a package wrapped in brown paper.

"Fabric?" Edie asked.

"Look and see."

Pulling the string off and tearing the paper away, Edie saw the most beautiful yellow dotted Swiss she'd ever laid her eyes on. "Oh, Lydia. It's beautiful!"

"I've watched that bolt ever since it first came in. I kept hoping a piece of it would land on the remnant table, and today it did! It'll certainly complement your dark hair. Keep looking. There's more," Lydia said, laughing. She removed her felt hat and hung it on the hook beside Mama's.

In the folds of the cloth were yards of fussy lace for the trim and a pattern for a dress. Edie was ready to explode with excitement. "But it's not my birthday or anything."

"Graduation's coming up," Lydia said.

Edie laughed. "Have you lost count? I don't graduate for three more years."

"Everyone wants to wear nice things on graduation night, whether you graduate or not." Lydia reached out to put her arm around Edie's shoulder. "Especially you!"

It was true. Edie loved pretty dresses. And with this lovely yellow dress, she could walk into Washington Elementary School on the night of graduation and know she'd look just as nice as someone like Sarah Whalen. Sarah's father owned a big shoe factory, and she always had the nicest clothes in all of fifth grade.

By the time supper was ready, Papa had come in, followed by Tim, who was finishing his junior year at Central High School. Edie loved this time of day when the whole family was crowded into their none-too-big kitchen, talking and laughing and sharing. They didn't have a big dining room like Aunt Frances and Uncle Richard, but Edie didn't care. This was home, and she loved it.

"Tim," Mama said, "would you go out and drag your brother out of that darkroom?"

"Yes, ma'am," Tim answered, moving toward the back door.

"And if Truman's still out there," she added, "be sure to invite him to stay for supper."

"He's probably hanging around just hoping you'd ask," Tim said with a grin. He winked at Lydia.

Edie wondered what that meant. She took her yellow fabric to the parlor and placed it atop the Franklin treadle sewing machine. Perhaps she and Lydia could pin the pattern and cut it out that very evening.

When she returned, Carl and Truman were washing up at the sink. She saw Truman take a peek at himself in the mirror above the sink. He slipped a comb from his pocket and slicked his hair back. His lean angular face, with the high chiseled cheekbones, was every bit as handsome as some of the actors Edie had seen in the flickers. Whereas Tim sported soft fuzz on his cheeks, Truman's whiskers looked a bit more bristly— as though he might truly shave each day.

Papa was next to step up to the sink as he attempted to get the white flour from the mill out of his hair and mustache. It was a hopeless battle.

Tim brought in a chair from the parlor and put it between his place and Lydia's, grinning all the while.

Papa was already asking Carl about the war news that had come in that day.

"The Battle of Verdun," Carl told him, "keeps dragging on and on. The only news is that the French are still holding on.

Who knows how much longer they can last?"

Edie remembered way back when all the fighting first started. Many people said it would be over in a few months. But now other countries had joined in, deep trenches had been dug throughout the countryside of France, and the entire war was in a hopeless deadlock. No one was winning, but thousands were dying.

Papa shook his head. "I cannot see how they can continue killing off all their finest young men. It is the annihilation of an entire generation. Senseless. So senseless."

"They thought the Brits would turn the tide," Tim said. "But it seems to have done nothing more than provide more targets for the German army."

"*We* could turn the tide," Truman said stiffly. "If President Wilson would agree to our fighting alongside the Allies, it would all be over in a whipstitch."

"Easy to say from this safe vantage point," Papa said softly.

Mama shooed everyone into their places. "What say we be seated and pray and thank God for this good food Edie prepared, before we get deep into war talk."

When Truman saw where his place was—right beside Lydia—he blushed to the tops of his ears. While Papa was praying, Edie peeked. Papa always prayed a long prayer before they ate, so she had plenty of time to look.

There it was, right in front of her eyes. Truman and Lydia were making sidelong glances at one another and smiling. Later, when the food was being passed, every time Lydia's hand brushed up against Truman's, he acted as though he'd touched a hot stove or something. When Lydia spoke directly to Truman, he stammered like a little school kid.

Edie tried not to laugh out loud. Why hadn't she noticed it before this? Truman Vaught was sweet on Lydia.

23

CHAPTER 4

God Is Faithful

Before leaving for home after supper, Truman asked Papa if he might join them at church the next morning. Papa smoothed his mustache, smiled, and said, "Any person is welcome in our church, Truman. You know that." He paused a moment. "But perhaps you are asking to sit with our family. Is that it?"

The tips of Truman's ears were pink again. "Well yes, sir. That is, if you don't mind."

"None of us minds in the least." Papa was sober as he added, "Attending a church where German is still spoken at times won't make you the most popular man in Minneapolis.

You are aware of that I presume?"

Truman nodded. "I've considered that, sir."

"Very well then. Come by first thing in the morning, and you may walk along with us."

"I will. And thank you, sir." With that Truman was out the door.

Later when Edie and Lydia were changing into their night-gowns in their small slant-ceilinged room upstairs, Edie asked, "Do you think Truman is in love with you?" It all seemed so romantic to Edie.

Lydia gave a shrug. "I have no idea, Edie. He's not said anything to me about it. But it's a bit soon to be talking about love, don't you think?" She pulled the hairpins from her pile of blond hair, and it spilled down around her shoulders. She took her hairbrush and counted each brush stroke aloud. Mama insisted the girls brush their hair one hundred strokes every night before going to bed. Lydia used to fuss and fume over such a thing, but now she did it without a murmur.

"I don't know about that. In the flickers the actors and actresses fall in love as soon as they see one another." Edie looked at the pictures of Mary Pickford and Florence Lawrence that she'd pinned on the wall by her side of their bed.

"I assure you, Edie. This isn't the flickers. This is just good old Lydia Schmidt who works in the basement of Woolworth's."

"You make it sound like nothing. I'm proud of you for having such a good job."

Lydia smiled. "I didn't mean it like that." She thought for a moment. "I'm thankful for my job, but it's quite small in comparison to what I dream of doing one day. And," she added, shaking her hairbrush to punctuate the words, "if the stars in the eyes of Truman Vaught might spoil my dreams and plans, then those stars don't move me one whit."

Edie knew Lydia meant what she said. Her older sister was so strong-headed and independent. "The only plan I have right now," Edie said, "is to win the spelling bee next week." She took her spelling book from the bureau. "Would you pronounce all the words from page 143 before we go to sleep?"

"Be glad to." Lydia fluffed the pillows behind her back and leaned against the head of the bed. She began with *antecedent*, going all the way to *zinnias*, and Edie spelled every word correctly.

The large stone church the Schmidts attended was only a few blocks from their house. Some Sundays they took the trolley, but on nice days they walked. Edie loved their church, especially the majestic tones of the pipe organ as it played the hymns that ministered peace and comfort to her each and every week. Although she wasn't sure why, she felt herself hoping Truman would like it as well.

As they entered the sanctuary, the strains of "Joyful, Joyful, We Adore Thee" swelled to fill every corner of the vast room and spilled out the open windows. The song was one of Edie's favorites. One reason she loved it was because it vibrated with joy and praise, and the other reason was because the composer was Ludwig van Beethoven, a German. Surely such beautiful music should prove to everyone that all Germans couldn't possibly be bad people.

Truman obviously wanted to sit beside Lydia, but she didn't make it easy for him. He wound up sitting between Tim and Carl. Edie didn't understand how Lydia could be that way. She was sure if a boy were sweet on her, she would probably swoon and faint dead away at his feet.

Pastor Moehr chose for his text that morning 2 Thessalonians 3:3, which said: *But the Lord is faithful, who shall stablish you, and keep you from evil.*

Edie could remember not long ago when all Scripture readings were read aloud in German, but that was being done less and less. That tradition was going by the way of the happy Biergartens where German families loved to gather on Sunday afternoons. Ever since the war began, anything that brought the German people together was frowned upon—even the athletic clubs and choral groups. Many of those groups had ceased to exist.

"The Lord is faithful," Pastor said, his voice booming from the raised platform where the pulpit stood. "It's a simple phrase but highly profound. You can trust in His faithfulness; you can count on His faithfulness." From there the pastor went on to recount examples in the Bible when God demonstrated His faithfulness. Like when Daniel was delivered from the mouths of lions. When Joseph was brought out of prison. When the angels helped Peter escape from prison. When Paul was saved from the shipwreck.

Edie knew each story by heart. She'd heard Papa tell them over and over again. Hearing the stories was easy; believing that God might do the same for her was much more difficult. Could He—would He—deliver her from the mean, ugly words the other children said to her at school each day?

Presently they stood to sing the closing hymn, "A Mighty Fortress Is Our God." Before they sang, Pastor said, "God wants to be your fortress today to protect and keep you."

Edie thought about that as she sang the words: *A mighty fortress is our God, A bulwark never failing; Our helper He, amid the flood Of mortal ills prevailing.* More than anything, she wanted to know God as her Fortress, her Helper.

Before the first verse was over, she detected movement down the pew. She looked just in time to see Truman deftly switching places with Carl so that he would be right next to Lydia. He took a corner of her hymnbook to sing from with her. Lydia was smiling. Edie figured if Truman kept at it, he might just make some progress with her older sister.

Tim had fun teasing Lydia about Truman as they walked to school together the next morning. Most girls would have blushed and denied any such thing, but not Lydia. She just laughed along with her brother, not denying a thing.

Lydia and Tim walked half of the way to school with Edie, then turned off to go to the high school. Sometimes Edie wished she could turn back time to last year, when Lydia was still at the elementary school with her. Somehow she always felt safer with Lydia by her side. This year, Carl wasn't with her, either.

Last June, Tim and Truman had fixed up an old bicycle and given it to Carl for his birthday gift. The bicycle meant he was able to throw a bigger newspaper route. It also meant he rode the bike to school, which made Edie feel more alone than ever.

If she truly had the power to turn back time, she'd turn it all the way back to the days before Papa became secretary of the labor union at the flour mill and before the war started. Most people in the city distrusted union men, and since the war, people also distrusted anyone with a German-sounding name. That meant Edie had been thrown smack dab in the middle of both.

When Papa first became an officer in the local labor union, someone had thrown a rock through the window in the front door of their house. Tied to the rock had been a threatening note. Edie remembered having nightmares after that happened. A few months ago, the Schmidts had had a telephone installed in their house, after which they received two phone calls threatening the family.

Papa prayed with them about it and told them that God would protect them from harm. Edie tried her best to believe that and she tried to forget the threats, but it wasn't easy. Sometimes scary thoughts crept in late at night right before she fell asleep. What if someone set fire to their house? Or what if someone tried to hurt Papa? That's when she would scoot closer to Lydia and snuggle up. But during school days, Edie was on her own.

Nell was at the schoolyard gate waiting for Edie when she arrived that morning. Just knowing Nell was her friend made each day at school a little easier. They fell into step as they walked over to the playground.

"You'll never guess what," Edie said in a cheerful voice. She didn't want to burden her best friend with her troubled thoughts, so she always tried to think of cheerful things to talk about. "Our friend from the newspaper, Truman Vaught, is sweet on Lydia."

Nell giggled. "You don't mean it. How do you know?"

"He stayed for supper Saturday evening and attended church with us yesterday. You should have seen him. Every time she so much as looked at him, he was all cotton-mouthed and bumfuzzled."

That comment sent them both into gales of laughter. As they sat on the seesaw, they talked about what it would be like to have a fellow actually pay attention to them, rather than teasing and tormenting them like all the boys did in grammar school.

"I'm sure we'll find out someday," Nell said.

The clanging bell sent the students scurrying to the front walk, where they lined up in rows to march into their class-rooms. In the fifth-grade room, students sat in assigned seats in alphabetical order, so Edie sat right in front of Nell. They loved being near one another but were careful not to talk and get into trouble.

Unfortunately Sarah Whalen sat in the next row, right across from Nell. Unfortunate because Sarah could do things behind Edie's back, like talk to Nell or pass notes to Nell. Sometimes Edie got a prickly sensation on the back of her neck as though Sarah were glaring at her.

"It's Michael's turn to hold the flag for the salute," Miss Hedley was saying, "but he's at home ill this morning. Do I have a volunteer?"

Edie's hand shot up in the air.

"Edith, didn't you hold the flag just a few days ago?" Miss Hedley was a strict, somber teacher with piercing gray-green eyes. Now those piercing eyes made Edie feel uncomfortable, but she wasn't going to back down.

"Yes, ma'am, I did. But I'd be pleased to hold it again."

"All right. Come forward."

Edie took the flag from its holder, walked to the center of the room near the teacher's desk, and held the flag high. "I pledge allegiance," she began in a strong voice. She was careful to keep her eyes on the Stars and Stripes and not glance out at Sarah or any of the other students. Surely they could see how much she loved her country by the way she was willing to hold the flag so often.

When the pledge was over, Miss Hedley went to the piano, and they sang the national anthem. Edie always sang louder than anyone. "What so proudly we hailed at the twilight's last gleaming." Somehow she wanted everyone to know just how much the flag meant to her. Then no one could dare call her a traitor.

CHAPTER 5

The Spelling Bee

At recess a group of girls had gathered to play jump rope with the large rope that was much longer than the individual, red-handled ones they played with by themselves. Two girls twirled the rope in time and chanted rhymes as girls ran in, jumped a certain number of times, and ran out again. The longer rope allowed the girls to jump two at a time.

Nell was as graceful as a gazelle, and she could skip rope longer than any girl in fifth grade and not miss.

"Come on," she said, pulling at Edie's arm. "Let's go in as a team."

Edie wanted to join in the fun, but the minute she saw Sarah at one end of the rope, she hesitated. Nell moved right into line to wait their turn. When she looked around to see Edie standing back, she reached out and grabbed her sleeve. "Move up here, Edie. Don't you want to jump with me?"

Edie moved up closer saying nothing.

The girls sang:

Solomon Grundy
  Born on Monday
Marries on Tuesday
  Took sick on Wednesday
Got worse on Thursday
  Dies on Friday
Buried on Saturday
  Then came Sunday and the end of Solomon Grundy

When the rhyme ended, the rope was twirled faster into "red-hot peppers" until someone missed. Happy laughter filled the air as the teams moved through and came around to get in line again. Then it was Nell and Edie's turn. Nell grabbed Edie's hand and said, "On the count of three, in we go. One, two, *three!*"

The two ran into the twirling rope in perfect rhythm, but just as they started jumping in time, the rope dropped at their feet.

"What's the matter?" Nell said. "We didn't miss. We were going great."

Edie knew Sarah was the one who had stopped twirling the rope first. She didn't dare look in Sarah's direction.

"I'll not lift a finger to turn this rope for a German traitor," Sarah said in a loud voice.

"Sarah Whalen," Nell said, "that's crazy talk, and you know it. Edie's our friend. She's not done anything wrong."

"She may be *your* friend," Sarah said. "And whether or not she's done anything wrong, none of us knows that for sure."

Edie leaned toward Nell and said softly, "You go ahead and jump. I'll go sit on the seesaw and watch."

"No, Edie. If you leave, I leave." Nell looked around at the other girls for a moment as though to dare them to oppose Sarah. None did.

The two spent the rest of recess on the seesaw and climbing on the jungle gym.

"You didn't have to leave on account of me," Edie said. The incident made her feel so ashamed.

"Yes I did. You're my friend," Nell stated firmly. "Friends stick together."

When school took up again, it was time for the spelling bee. Edie had been so upset over Sarah's words on the playground, she wasn't sure she could stand up in front of the class and take part in the spelling bee. But no one had a choice. Miss Hedley had all the students in the room stand up around the edge of the classroom. Students who missed a word took their seat. The last person standing would be the winner.

Miss Hedley began the contest with relatively simple words—ones that were found in the front of their fifth-grade speller. Edie's first word was *inclement,* which was easy as pie. In spite of the simple words, several students went down during the first round.

Edie's second word was *versatile,* and again she had no trouble. Nell lost out in the fifth round, missing the word *incredible* because she used the suffix *-able* rather than *-ible.* Edie was sorry to see her friend go because the two of them had been standing side by side. Every time Edie was given a word, Sarah stared at her with a glare that bore right through her.

Finally there were only four students standing—two boys, Sarah Whalen, and Edie.

"Edith Schmidt," Miss Hedley said, "spell *philosophy*."

"Philosophy. P-h-i-l-o-s-o-p-h-y. Philosophy."

"Correct. Randall, spell *solicitous.*"

Randall thought a moment and then thought some more.

When Miss Hedley began to count backward, "Five, four, three. . ." everyone knew Randall had to begin spelling or be disqualified.

"Solicitous," Randall said. "S-o-l-i-s-i-t-o-u-s. Solicitous."

Turning to Edie, Miss Hedley pronounced the word again.

Edie took a slow breath, pronounced the word aloud, and then spelled it correctly. Randall glumly took his seat.

During the next round, the second boy, Farley, missed *supererogatory*. Now it was between Sarah and Edie. Edie wiped the sweaty palms of her hands down her white pinafore. Her next word was *obsequious*. She paused long enough to try to envision the word from that page in her speller. Was it *qui* or *que*? "Five, four," Miss Hedley began.

"Obsequious," Edie said slowly. "O-b-s-e-q-u-i-o-u-s. Obsequious." She held her breath until she heard Miss Hedley say, "Correct, Edith," then she released a quiet sigh.

Now it was back to Sarah. Her word was *imperturbable*.

Throughout the contest, Edie had kept her eyes away from Sarah because of the way Sarah was glaring at her. Looking at those unkind eyes would only have made her more uncomfortable. But now there was a quiet pause, so Edie looked. Sarah's face clearly revealed that she was stumped.

Miss Hedley waited as long as she could, then she began counting backward from five.

"Imperturbable," Sara said. "I-m-p-e-r-t-e-r-b-a-b-l-e. Imperturbable."

Suddenly Edie felt a warm glow beginning from her high-top button shoes and rising to wash over her head. She must not smile. She must not gloat. Miss Hedley turned to Edie and repeated the word. "Edith, spell *imperturbable*."

"Imperturbable. I-m-p-e-r-t-u-r-b-a-b-l-e. Imperturbable."

"Correct," Miss Hedley said with little excitement. "Edith Schmidt is our new spelling champion."

Sarah shot Edie a hate-filled look as she returned to her seat. Nell was clapping her hands. A few others did as well, but not many. After all, how would it look if they cheered for a girl with a German name like Schmidt?

But Edie didn't care. She'd won fair and square. As she sat down, she heard Sarah say, "The dirty Hun probably cheated." To which Nell whispered back, "You're just a sore loser, Sarah Whalen."

Edie appreciated the way Nell stood up for her, but how she wished there were no need for Nell to have to do such a thing at all.

If the fifth-grade class was less than enthusiastic over Edie's win, her family made up for it. That night at supper when she told them what had happened, they were jubilant and showered her with congratulations. She could see the special pride in Mama's and Papa's eyes. Papa reached out and patted her hand. "Our star pupil," he said.

"I knew when you were spelling the words last evening that you knew them all," Lydia said. "I knew you could do it."

"It takes a cool head to spell correctly in front of all the other students," Carl added.

Edie knew Carl hated being in front of other people and

avoided it at all costs. She didn't like it much herself, especially in front of Sarah.

"Now what?" Mama wanted to know. "Is there yet another contest?"

Edie nodded as she rose to fetch more bread from the warming oven and placed it on the table in front of Papa. "I compete against the winners of the sixth, seventh, and eighth grades. The contest will be the last week of school."

"I'll help pronounce words every evening if you like," Lydia offered.

"Tell me again the name of the girl you beat," Papa said.

"Her name is Whalen. Sarah Whalen," Edie answered.

"Her papa it is who owns Whalen's Boots and Shoes, am I correct?" Papa said.

Edie nodded. She had said little to Mama and Papa about the bad things that happened at school. She didn't want to worry them, since they had enough to be concerned about. So in answering Papa, she made no unkind remarks about Sarah. Instead she said, "Sarah's papa's factory is helping the Allies to win the war."

"Oh," Timothy said, suddenly becoming interested in the conversation. "How is he doing that?"

"Sarah says the factory has received large orders for military boots for British soldiers," Edie explained. She'd heard Sarah brag about it unceasingly. "Soldiers with good boots make better fighters, she says."

Tim shook his head. "That's not helping to win the war. That's just helping Mr. Whalen to become rich *because* of the war."

"Timothy," Mama warned in her sternest voice. "We'll not speak unkindly of others. I'm sure if we owned a shoe factory, we'd fill those orders just as Mr. Whalen is doing."

"Perhaps," Timothy replied. "But we wouldn't twist the truth to say we were doing it to help win the war."

Edie thought about that as she finished her supper. Other people said unkind things whenever the mood hit them, but in their house Mama and Papa strictly forbade it. How different the world would be if all people were like Mama and Papa.

Chapter 6
Frosty

The lilac bushes in Aunt Frances's yard were in full bloom. The thick lavender clusters waved in the spring breeze like a lovely lady waving her perfumed wrist. The fragrance filled the air as the cousins played in the spring sunshine.

The grown-ups were sitting in the rocking chairs on the front porch talking about serious things such as war and politics. A presidential election was approaching, and they often discussed whether or not Wilson would run again, and if he did, whether he could be elected.

Carl and Edie and Nell had been playing tag with the little ones, but now they all sat on the porch steps, drinking lemonade and eating cookies. They'd even allowed little Harry to join in their games.

The two families spent most every Saturday evening together. Carl and Edie would go over early in the afternoon, then the other members of the family arrived as they got off work, taking the trolley to the Allerton home. Edie welcomed the Saturday visits because it meant she could spend more time with Nell.

"When we finish with our snack," Nell said, "let's play with the kittens."

"Oh let's do." Edie drained the last of the tart lemonade in her tall glass. The kittens' eyes were now open, and they were cute little balls of fluff. The one with gray fur tipped in white she had named Frosty. "It looks as though he's covered in white frost," she'd told Nell. Edie had been trying to muster up the courage to ask Mama if she could have Frosty for her very own.

As the girls finished their snacks, they took the tray and went about gathering up the glasses for Aunt Frances. Just then the telephone rang from inside the front hallway.

"Probably Mrs. Kilpatrick ready to have that baby," Uncle Richard remarked as he set his glass on the tray. Uncle Richard was often called away on emergencies in the middle of their visits. Sometimes it would interrupt the grown-ups' game of whist, which they often played together.

Nell and Edie followed Aunt Frances into the house, taking the tray of glasses back to the kitchen. From down the hallway, Edie could hear her aunt's excited voice saying, "Oh, Esther! It's you! How good to hear your voice again. How are you?"

"She sounds excited," Nell said as they put the glasses into the sink. "Who's Esther?"

"My aunt from down in Missouri. She's Mama and Uncle Richard's younger sister. Come on, let's see what she wants."

Edie led the way back down the wide hall to where Aunt Frances stood talking to her sister-in-law. It must have been a wretched connection because Aunt Frances had to keep asking Aunt Esther to repeat what she'd said. Then Aunt Frances kept repeating what she'd said. Even from where Edie was standing, she could hear the crackling static on the phone line.

After a moment, Aunt Frances covered the mouthpiece and said to Edie, "Go tell Uncle Richard to come here. Tell him Esther and Erik are coming home!"

Edie did as she was told, and soon Uncle Richard was talking over the sound of crackling static to Uncle Erik—something about Uncle Richard finding a house for them in the neighborhood.

Excitement stirred inside Edie as she listened. Aunt Esther and Uncle Erik had left Minneapolis four years ago, and none of the rest of the family had even seen their daughter, three-year-old Adeline.

Nell grabbed Edie's hand. "What wonderful news," she said, "to have the rest of your family coming home."

Nell always seemed to understand.

"Are they truly coming back?" Edie asked Uncle Richard the moment he hung up the receiver. "Are Aunt Esther and Uncle Erik coming back here to live?"

Uncle Richard put his arm about her shoulder. "Questions, questions, too many questions," he teased. "Come on outside, and I'll tell everyone the news at one time."

It was true. The Moes were moving back in June. Even Mama seemed excited, and quiet Mama seldom became visibly excited. "Why, they'll be here before the Fourth of July," she said. "Perhaps we could have a family picnic together."

"A splendid idea," Aunt Frances agreed. "Let's have it right here in our backyard."

"Erik wants me to find a house for them in this area," Uncle Richard said as he sat back down in the rocking chair. "He says he'll be mighty pleased to be back in the city again. He's had his fill of farm life."

Uncle Erik had never been too keen on going to Missouri in the first place, but his aging aunt and uncle needed him there. It was duty that called him rather than the benefits of country living. Edie remembered two years ago at Christmas when a letter from them said that his uncle had died. Now his aunt had passed on as well.

"Did they have any trouble selling the farm?" Aunt Frances asked.

"Not at all," Uncle Richard answered. "It fetched a fine price, too, which tells me that Erik must have had the place in fairly good working order in spite of his citified ways."

"I think they hired good workers," Aunt Frances put in.

"What's he planning to do?" Papa asked. "I could maybe get him on at the mill."

Uncle Richard shook his head. "No need, Hans. He's already in contact with the Minneapolis *Tribune*. A job is waiting for him there."

Lydia's ears perked up. "He'll be working where Truman works."

Edie smiled. For a girl who was trying to act as though a boy didn't matter, Lydia seemed to always be thinking about Truman Vaught.

Nell leaned over to Edie just then and whispered, "We were going to play with the kittens when the telephone rang. Remember?"

"You're right, we were." The adult's conversation was

getting a little boring anyway. "Let's go."

In the shed, the girls lifted the wooden apple crate full of mewing kittens and carried it out into the grassy yard. One by one they lifted the babies out of the crate and let them navigate through the grass. It was funny to see them crawling around. Gloria and Larry ran from where they were playing to join the fun.

"Mama says we're to begin finding homes for them next week," Gloria said as she held up the black kitten and kissed the top of its head.

"Next week?" Edie picked up Frosty and stroked his back with her finger. "That's awfully soon."

"She says they're ready."

"Mama says I may have one," Nell said.

"Which one will you take?" Larry wanted to know. "You get first pick you know."

"Do I?" Nell said.

Edie held her breath hoping Nell wouldn't want Frosty. But she said, "I like the little calico—the female. I'll call her Callie." She looked at Edie. "Are you taking one, too?"

"I haven't asked yet."

Nell smiled. "You'd like to have Frosty, wouldn't you?"

"You're so perceptive," Edie said smiling.

"That's not perceptive," Larry said. "Anyone with eyes could see you like him the best."

Edie laughed. She guessed her feelings had been pretty plain. Frosty was coming toward her through the grass. She picked him up and cuddled him in her hands. He was always so docile and quiet. She was sure he'd make a great pet.

As the family rode the trolley back to their house that evening, everyone was talking about the Moe family returning to Minneapolis. Mama seemed so happy. Edie thought it was the perfect time to ask about Frosty. When they disembarked the trolley and walked the block and a half to the house, she made sure she was walking by Mama's side.

"Aunt Frances is going to begin giving away the kittens next week," she began cautiously.

"Already?" Mama said. "It seems just yesterday that they were born."

"Nell's mama is letting her have one of them."

Papa and the boys were walking ahead of them, talking among themselves. Lydia was on the other side of Mama.

Then, just as though Edie hadn't said a thing, Lydia said, "Isn't it a coincidence that Carl throws papers for the *Tribune*, Truman works in the darkroom there, and now Uncle Erik will be a reporter there as well? We'll be surrounded by newspaper people."

There she went, talking about Truman again. "Lydia, you interrupted me," Edie said, feeling miffed.

Lydia looked around Mama at her little sister. "No, I didn't. You were finished talking."

"I may have been finished with one sentence, but I wasn't done with the subject."

"Edie," Mama said gently, "that's not a very nice tone to use with your sister."

"Well, she should listen to others before speaking," Edie said.

"I've not known Lydia to be insensitive to others," Mama countered.

Edie thought about her new yellow dress that was nearly finished, and a wave of guilt swept over her. Mama was right. Lydia wasn't insensitive. "I'm sorry," Edie said. "I didn't mean that, Lydia."

"I accept your apology," Lydia said softly. "What was it

you wanted to say?"

Knowing that now she'd probably never get to have a kitten, Edie stumbled over her request to Mama. "One of the Allertons' kittens is fluffier than all the rest, and he seems to like me. He has silvery-gray fur, tipped in white. Nell says she's never seen such a pretty-colored kitten in all her life."

"Is that the one she picked?" Lydia asked.

"No," Edie replied. "She wants the calico. The silver-gray one is my favorite. I've named him Frosty." She paused a moment. "Oh, Mama, may I please have Frosty for my own? I'll take such good care of him. I promise I will. He won't be a bit of trouble for anyone. School will be out soon, and I'll have time to train him and take care of him—"

"Whoa," Papa said over his shoulder. "What's this talk I hear?"

"Edie is asking if she may have one of the Allerton kittens," Mama told him.

"A cat?" Carl spoke up then. "I've had mice in the shed. A cat would be great for out there."

"Oh, no," Edie said quickly. "Not in the shed. Then it would be your cat, not mine."

"You seem to be very strongly set about this," Mama said.

Edie thought about that a moment. She wanted the little kitten more than she'd realized. "I've spent time with him every time I've been at their house. I guess I've grown attached to him."

"I could help her take care of him," Lydia said. Edie could have hugged her.

"But you're not home very much," Mama said.

"When I am there I can help," Lydia assured her.

Edie knew she could take care of the cat all by herself, but it was nice of Lydia to offer.

At last Mama said she and Papa would talk about it and let her know. Edie released a long sigh. What if Frosty was given away before Mama and Papa even made up their minds? That was the chance she had to take. At least they hadn't said no.

CHAPTER 7
Edie's Surprise

Lydia and Edie sewed lace on the yellow dress by hand, using tiny precise stitches. Knowing how much Lydia disliked hand-work made Edie appreciate all the more her sister's efforts. The dress had a drop waist and full pleated skirt with lace all about the big square collar and on the fitted cuffs. From the scrap pieces, the two girls created a large bow for the back of Edith's hair.

One night after they had worked several hours on the dress, the two girls were getting ready for bed when Edie thanked Lydia for all her hard work on the dress. "It's going to be as pretty as any dress there," she said as she slipped into her flannel nightgown. Soon it would be warm enough to pack the flannels away in the cedar chest, but the early mornings were still quite cool.

"We want you to look your best when you accept your spelling bee award."

Edie laughed. "But I haven't won the spelling bee yet, silly."

"Well, hand me the speller, and let's make sure you do."

Lydia had dug about in her old things and pulled out copies of her old spelling workbooks from seventh and eighth grades. Those were the ones Lydia was using now to pronounce the words to Edie. Edie wasn't sure she had any chance at all against the older students. When she said that to Tim once, he told her she had every bit as good a chance as anyone else. All she needed to do was believe in herself.

That was easy for Tim to say. Both he and Lydia were full of confidence, but Edie wasn't at all like her older siblings. Nevertheless, every night she and Lydia went through the pages of the spellers until neither girl could hold her eyes open.

The spelling bee was held the last week of school. The event took place in the school auditorium in front of the entire student body of Washington Elementary. All morning, Edie's stomach was churning and rolling and she could barely eat lunch.

"Don't worry," Nell said to her. "You'll do fine. Look at it this way, even if you don't win, you'll at least have gotten farther than anyone else in our class. Even farther than Sarah Whalen." Then she added, "And I'll be right there rooting for you."

The kind words were appreciated but did little to settle Edie's stomach. By the time she was seated on the stage that afternoon, she could barely swallow because her mouth and throat were so dry. How would she ever be able to speak?

The auditorium had been decorated for graduation. Crepe paper streamers and yards of crimson bunting adorned the stage, along with large white wicker baskets that would later be filled with fresh-cut spring flowers. From her position on the stage, Edie could see Nell. Farther toward the back she could see Carl's face. Even though Carl hadn't said much, she knew he was proud of her.

The bee opened up with easy words like *odious* and *laxity* and moved on to more difficult ones such as *palliation* and *labyrinth*. For several rounds no one missed a word. Mr. Dunning, the eighth-grade teacher, pronounced the words, and he did so quite distinctly. Edie's nervousness began to lessen somewhat. She managed to concentrate on every word and to take her time.

All of a sudden, the girl from seventh grade missed a word. This was more of a shock to Edie than if she herself had missed. Now there were only three contestants, she and the two boys, one from sixth and the other from eighth grade.

As Edie watched the seventh-grade girl take her seat, her eyes caught Sarah's. In a flash, Sarah made an ugly face, crossing her eyes, wrinkling her nose, and sticking out her tongue. It was ghastly. As if on cue, Edie's stomach began the familiar pitching and rolling once again.

Just as a new round was to begin, the side door of the auditorium opened. In walked Mama, followed by Timothy and Lydia. They paused a moment, looked up at her and smiled, and then quietly slipped into seats near the back.

Mama taking time off from work? That was unheard of. Mama never missed a day of work and never took off for anything but the most dire emergencies. Yet there she was. She must have arranged for Lydia and Tim to get out of school for their last hour. From that moment, nothing Sarah Whalen could have done would have upset Edie. She pretended it was Lydia pronouncing the words to her, going through the seventh- and eighth-grade spellers as they had night after night. On she went through *unctuous* and *pamphleteer,* never missing a word. At last the sixth-grade boy missed *voyager,* and there were only two students left.

Edie felt Lydia smiling at her, and she relaxed knowing that now, whether she won or lost, she'd still made her family proud of her. She easily spelled *martyrize,* after which Mr. Dunning pronounced *wainscoting*.

"Wainscoting," said Luther, the eighth grader. Edie darted a glance over at him. It was obvious he was puzzled. Hesitating just a moment, he plunged in, "W-a-i-n-s-c-o-t-t-i-n-g. Wainscoting."

Mr. Dunning turned to Edie. The moment he pronounced *wainscoting* one more time, everyone knew Luther had mis-spelled it. If Edie also missed it, Luther would have another chance at a new word, and the contest would continue.

Edie looked at Lydia. Lydia smiled. Edie took a breath. "Wainscoting," she repeated. "W-a-i-n-s-c-o-t-i-n-g. Wainscoting."

"Correct!" Mr. Dunning said in a loud voice. "Edith Schmidt is the official winner of the 1916 Washington Elementary School spelling bee!"

The eighth graders groaned loudly, but the fifth graders were cheering. Edie felt as though her heart were going to burst right out of her chest. Miss Hedley presented her with a gold-plated loving cup and pinned an award ribbon to the collar of her dress, then shook her hand and said, "Congratulations."

Edie could hardly remember what happened after that. As she came down off the stage, Nell was there hugging her, and then her family surrounded her, making her feel as though she were the most special person in the whole world. And for a moment, she truly was. Surely this would prove to the whole school that Germans were not bad.

The six Schmidts walked to the elementary school together the night of graduation. As they stepped out of their house, Mrs. Bierschwale was weeding the flowers that bordered her front porch. "Ach, a fine-looking family it is, the Schmidts," she said.

"Good evening, Mrs. Bierschwale," Papa said, tipping his best Sunday hat.

Mrs. Bierschwale stood and wiped her muddy hands on her apron. "Ja, the Lydia even is a lady now. And little Edie, almost grown, she is." Their neighbor clucked her tongue. "Goes by too fast, the time does."

"The children do grow up in a hurry," Mama said politely. In spite of the fact that Mrs. Bierschwale was rather bossy and sometimes nosy, Mama and Papa had taught the children to always treat her with respect.

Mrs. Bierschwale turned back to her weeding then, and the family continued on. The balmy evening air was sweet with the aroma of spring flowers. Edie fairly floated down the sidewalk, feeling regal in her new yellow dress with the starched bow in the back of her hair. She repeatedly thanked Lydia for purchasing the fabric and sewing the dress. Carl teased her and called her a canary, but Edie didn't mind a bit.

Truman Vaught had been invited to attend as well. He walked beside Timothy and Papa. As usual Truman was talking about the war. "Have you heard about the American Field Ambulance?" he said to no one in particular.

"There was an article in the *Tribune* about it," Carl

answered. Carl read everything in the papers. Carl read everything, period. Edie never saw a boy who read as much as Carl did.

"You read about it?" Truman seemed delighted that Carl knew what he was talking about. "What do you think about such a thing?" he wanted to know. "Isn't it a swell idea? Americans going over there to drive ambulances and helping with the wounded French and British soldiers."

"Sounds frightening to me," Lydia said.

"I must agree," Papa said solemnly.

"But it's a way we can assist," Truman said. "A small way that we can show the Allies that we believe in their cause. At least until slow old President Wilson decides to declare war."

"Slow to speak, slow to anger is scriptural, my son," Papa said in his kindest voice.

"But we've been slow to do both," Truman countered. "How much slower do we have to be?"

"Why would anyone be in a hurry to be shot at? Or to die?" Carl put in.

"Some things are worth risking your life for," Truman replied.

The way in which Truman said it made Edie think perhaps he truly believed those words. It gave her a little shiver to think of people dying and suffering over there on those faraway battlefields.

"Why are we talking about sober, serious things on such a glorious night?" she asked.

"Yes, why?" Lydia echoed.

"I agree," Mama said. "Let's talk about how nice Edie looks and how proud we are of her for winning the spelling bee."

Mama's gentle words chased the shivers away and made Edie feel safe and loved.

Having come in their new Hupmobile, Aunt Frances and Uncle Richard were in their seats when the Schmidts arrived. Harry was already squirming and wanting to get down from his chair. Edie slipped in beside him and put him on her lap, which calmed him somewhat. Aunt Frances smiled at her.

Across the aisle sat Nell with her mother and father. Her organza dress was the color of the lilacs in Aunt Frances's backyard, and she too had a large bow in the back of her hair. The two girls exchanged smiles and waved at one another. While Edie sometimes envied the wealth in Nell's family, still she knew she wouldn't want to trade places. She would never want to give up her big, happy, supportive family.

Amid all the speeches and special musical numbers, awards were presented to students for various accomplishments. Both Gloria and Larry received awards for having high grades in their classes. They were very good students. Finally the presentation was made to Edie for being the best speller in the entire school.

As her name was called, Edie set Harry down and stood to her feet. "Me go wiff Edie!" Harry proclaimed loudly, waving his teddy in the air. His antics made the audience twitter and made Edie blush. Aunt Frances shushed him and pulled him up onto her lap.

Edie stepped forward and up onto the stage to receive her certificate for having won the school spelling bee. Everyone clapped, but her family clapped louder than anyone else. She glanced out at them and smiled.

When the ceremonies were over, Uncle Richard offered to take them all home in his new automobile. The Hupmobile was a deep rich burgundy with shiny chrome trim. It looked nothing like the old black Model T Ford that he used to have.

It was a tight squeeze, but they all fit in with Larry sitting on Tim's lap, Gloria on Lydia's, and Harry on Aunt Frances's. Papa teased that he could put Carl on his lap, and everyone laughed. Carl said he could ride on the running board like they did in the *Keystone Cops* flickers.

Before Uncle Richard started the engine, he said, "Wait just a minute. What's that I hear?"

All the talking instantly quieted.

"I don't hear anything," Gloria said, then she giggled. "What do you hear, Papa?"

"Why, just listen," Uncle Richard said.

Again everyone was quiet. Again Gloria giggled. Larry shushed her.

Then Edie heard it. A tiny mew. "Why, it sounds like a kitten. Did one of the kittens crawl up into your car?"

"Perhaps one did," Aunt Frances said. "Perhaps a kitten crawled up into our Hupmobile—" She leaned over and picked up a small pasteboard box from the floor of the car. "To go home with a very special little girl who just happens to be the best speller in all of Washington Elementary School."

With that, she handed the box into the back seat to Edie.

Edie held her breath as she heard another protesting mew. Carefully she unfolded the flaps of the box. There inside was Frosty!

"Surprise!" Gloria said with a squeal. "It's your surprise!"

Gently Edie lifted the beautiful fluffy kitten out of the box and onto her lap. She looked over at Mama. "May I keep him?"

Mama smiled and reached over to pet the kitten. "You may. We all decided this would be the best gift to give to you for your special evening."

"Oh, thank you. All of you. Thank you so much." She lifted the kitten to rub its fur against her cheek. It was soft and warm and smelled the good smell of baby kittens. Her very own kitten. It was like a dream come true.

CHAPTER 8

Carl to the Rescue

The beautiful summer lay ahead of Edie like pages of a happy storybook. Aunt Frances had hired her to be a mother's helper three afternoons a week, which meant not only would she be earning her own money, but she'd be able to see Nell all summer.

That, plus the fact that Aunt Esther and Uncle Erik were coming in a few weeks, amounted to more good things than Edie had known for a long time. And best of all, Frosty was her very own. He followed her everywhere and slept on the bed at her feet every night.

Frosty's antics kept the entire family in uproarious laughter. He played with balls of Mama's knitting wool or with empty wooden spools. Lacking that, he played with his own shadow or the cords on the drapery. He needed so little to keep him occupied. Edie loved him more with each passing day. She and Nell compared notes as to how their kittens were growing and learning.

Aunt Frances was grateful that she could get away from the house without having to ask Dory, the cook, to watch the children. "After all, I did hire her to cook," she said, "and not to be a nanny."

Larry still wasn't too happy about having Edie as his keeper, but since he was off playing with neighborhood boys most of the time, it didn't matter as much.

One sunny June afternoon, Edie and Nell were playing paper dolls with Gloria on the front porch. The air was still and hot, with not enough breeze to ruffle the piles of paper dolls.

"Let's have our ladies dress up and go to the hotel for Sunday brunch," Gloria said.

"Oh, I like that idea," Nell agreed. "Here," she said as she sorted out the fanciest dresses, "let's make them look splendid."

Because Nell's father worked as a jeweler for a big jewelry store downtown, sometimes Nell truly did eat at the restaurant in the West Hotel. Edie had never even been inside a hotel, let alone eaten in one.

There were enough dolls so each girl could take one and dress it in dainty slippers, fur-trimmed coats, and fancy hats. Edie constantly kept an eye on Harry, who was playing with his toys a little way off. Earlier, Harry had stepped right in the middle of the paper dolls and almost torn Gloria's favorite doll.

"Me play, too," he'd begged. "Me play."

"No, Harry," Edie told him. "These are Gloria's paper dolls. You might tear them." Then she picked him up bodily and moved him back to his own place where his toys were. "You play with Harry's toys."

He cried for a moment or two, but she quickly showed him how to load his wooden blocks onto his toy train and play choo-choo. Then she returned to the paper dolls. The paper dolls were beautifully done in bright colors, and Edie loved playing with them.

After the dolls went to the hotel for brunch, Nell suggested they attend a ball. Now the fur-lined coats came off and the elegant ball gowns were chosen.

"I know what," Gloria said. "Let's move the Victrola over near the front door and put on a waltz record. It'll be as though our girls are dancing to a real orchestra."

"That's such a good idea," Nell said. Turning to Edie she said, "You certainly have a creative cousin."

Edie saw the six-year-old basking in Nell's praise. It was obvious Gloria adored Nell.

"Would your papa mind if we moved the Victrola into the front hall?" Nell asked.

"If we moved our game to the other side of the porch nearer the front parlor," Edie suggested, "we wouldn't have to move it far at all. We'll move the dolls first. Then I'll get Harry and his toys."

That decided, they began to quickly gather up the dolls. They moved them from the front of the house to the side of the house and again spread out the paper dolls and their dresses.

"I'll go in and wind up the Victrola," Gloria volunteered, "since it was my idea."

Once the dramatic strains of the "Blue Danube Waltz"

were drifting out the window from the Victrola, their dolls had a wonderful time at the formal ball.

All of a sudden, Edie said, "Oh, no! I nearly forgot to bring Harry around with us." As she stood up, a mournful yowl sounded from Harry's direction. Hurrying to the front, she saw Harry on the porch steps with his head through the wooden rails that supported the stair banister.

"Harry Allerton, get your head out of there this instant," she commanded. But it was obvious that Harry could not obey. His head was stuck. He was struggling for all he was worth and crying as he did so.

"Janelle, come help me!" Edie cried.

Nell and Gloria were instantly by her side.

"Harry, you little dickens," Gloria scolded. "Just wait'll Mama hears about this."

"Now don't get excited, Gloria," Edie said. "Maybe Aunt Frances doesn't need to be bothered about this little thing. We'll have him out of there in just a minute." Edie couldn't believe what this toddler could do the moment her back was turned. Hadn't she learned her lesson with the molasses incident?

"I'm not so sure we can do this," Nell said with foreboding in her voice. "He seems to be really stuck."

Now Harry was beginning to panic, and he was crying harder. Edie sat on the steps by his side and spoke calmly to him, trying to still his cries. "Now, now, Harry. Don't cry. We'll have you out of there in no time."

Nell went into the thick spirea bushes beside the steps to get on the other side where Harry's head was sticking through. She tried to gently push his head back through, but he cried harder.

"It's no use," she said. "We may need to call the fire department."

Edie gasped at the thought. She could just see it. Her picture on the front page of the *Tribune* with the headline "Neglectful Mother's Helper Causes Injury to Hapless Toddler."

Just then she heard a bell. A bicycle bell. Turning around, she saw Carl riding up the walk. Never had she been so happy to see anyone in all her life.

"Carl!" she cried out. "Come help us."

"What's happened?" he said, jumping off his bicycle and letting it land in the grass. "Sounds like he's dying!"

"His head's stuck. We can't get it out," she explained over the sound of Harry's cries.

Before Carl could fairly assess the situation, Larry appeared. "I knew it," he said to Edie. "I knew you wouldn't be a very good mother's helper."

Edie withered under his attack, but Carl put a hand on his young cousin's shoulder. "Larry, that's rather unkind. I came over here to help you learn to ride my bicycle."

That quieted Larry good and proper. Edie was terribly thankful that her big brother had arrived.

He instructed Nell to support Harry's head and told Edie to hold the little boy's stocky body across her lap. "Get him as level as possible. Then we'll go from there," he told them.

Harry was kicking and thrashing and pulling. Carl spoke gently to Harry, "Hey, there, little man. Quiet down now and be brave. Cousin Carl will have you out of here quick's a cat can wink her eye."

Harry sniffled a little and looked hopefully at Carl. Carl studied the wooden posts and gently tried to maneuver the toddler's head back through the space. "If it came in, surely it will go out again." But as he increased the pressure, Harry resumed crying.

His next idea was for Larry to bring out the lard can.

59

"Perhaps if we grease him up a little, he'll slide through."

"Oh, Carl," Edie said, "that's a wonderful idea."

But that didn't work either. By now they were all quite frustrated.

"Larry, go to your father's workbench down in the basement and bring me a hammer."

"Wow," Larry said, "are you going to hammer his head out of there?"

"Of course not!" Carl said. "Now hurry."

Carl was so smart. With the hammer he tapped at the banister. That made it lift enough to move one of the posts over. All that was needed was a fraction of an inch, and with one good shove from Nell and a squeal from Harry, the little boy's head was free at last!

Edie cuddled Harry for a moment, getting lard all over the front of her pinafore. It seemed that being around Harry meant there was always a mess of some kind. "I'll go wash him up and put him in bed for a nap," she said.

Carl told the others that there was no need to mention the incident to anyone—to which they all agreed. Edie appreciated his concern, but he could have saved his breath. Harry himself spilled the beans.

A clean and rested Harry met his mama when she arrived home. Immediately he pointed to the porch railing and said, "Harry caught in dere. Hurt, ow-ee," and proceeded to rub his neck and head. Red raw places just beneath his ears showed clearly where they'd tried to pull him out.

There was nothing to do but tell Aunt Frances the whole story. Again Edie was admonished not to let the little guy out of her sight. Then Aunt Frances kindly added, "But he could have put his head in there if you'd been sitting right beside him."

When Carl told the story at supper that evening, Tim

thought it quite funny. "That little character is always into some type of mischief. It must be his personality!"

Mama agreed with a smile. "Some children are just that way," she added.

But all the understanding from her family didn't help Edie feel any better about the situation. She wanted so much to do a good job for Aunt Frances and to be a responsible worker like Tim and Lydia and Carl all were.

The Moe family was due to arrive late in June. Uncle Richard had located a bungalow for them a few blocks from the Allertons' home. "A perfect fit," he told them, "for a little family like theirs."

Papa was as pleased as the rest of them that the family group was growing. Edie wondered if Papa missed being with his own German kinfolk. Sometimes weeks and months would pass before he spoke to his brothers and cousins. It had been almost two years since Papa had decided to stop taking part in the festivities and social events of the Minneapolis German community. Back then, many Germans were supportive of the actions of Kaiser Wilhelm, and Papa could not abide by that kind of stand.

Edie remembered the night when Papa spoke to them at family prayer time and announced he would no longer be a member of the German-American Alliance, nor would he attend German festivals "as long as my fellow Germans condone the barbaric action occurring in the country of Belgium."

It was a brave stand for Papa to take. But by the time the German Americans stopped supporting the violence of the Kaiser, many of the German groups were no longer gathering together. In fact, several of the large Biergartens had closed.

It was no wonder that Papa enjoyed their times at the

Allertons so much and why he was looking forward to the arrival of the Moe family.

When it was time to go to the train station to pick up Uncle Erik and Aunt Esther, there wasn't room for everyone to go. But Aunt Frances agreed to stay behind with Harry. "Dory and I will have dinner on when you return," she told them. To Mama she said, "Anna, you go on and see your sister. You need to be there."

Then Tim and Carl also agreed to stay at the Allertons so there would be more room in the automobile. Edie didn't want to offer to stay behind. She wanted very much to be right there when her little cousin and aunt and uncle stepped off that train.

Crowds of people were coming and going in the vast Minneapolis railway station when they arrived. Edie shivered with excitement at the sounds of the huffing trains coming to a stop at the various gates. Uncle Richard stepped over to one of the ticket windows to ask at which gate the train from Kansas City would be arriving.

"This way," he said as he ushered their little group down a long hallway. "Gate 23."

"There it is," Larry piped up. "See, it says Gate 23."

"And there's the train," Gloria added.

Sure enough, the train was at that moment pulling into the station and coming to a stop. Uncle Richard led them out onto the platform where they could watch the passengers get off.

Suddenly, Uncle Erik appeared, waving and calling. He looked all dapper in a lightweight linen suit and straw boater. His handlebar mustache was turned and waxed precisely at the tips in curls the size of quarters. Edie had to agree with Uncle Richard. This man didn't look at all like a farmer—except for his calloused hands.

Aunt Esther hugged Mama and fussed over the children

exclaiming how big each one had grown. The fitted bottle-green suit she wore reflected perfectly her smiling green eyes. Edie hadn't remembered that Aunt Esther was so much taller than Mama, nor that she was so pretty.

After receiving hugs from her aunt and uncle, Edie looked down at her cousin Adeline, who was dressed all in ruffles and lace and whose ivory skin and jet black hair made her look like a Dresden doll. Edie knelt down in front of Adeline and said, "Hello, Adeline. I'm your cousin Edith. But you can call me Edie."

Adeline batted her long eyelashes, put her finger in her mouth, and stared, saying nothing. Edie was smitten. Her cousin was the most darling little girl she'd ever seen.

CHAPTER 9

Family United

The Tuesday after Uncle Erik and Aunt Esther arrived was the Fourth of July. Edie had so much to be happy about she was near to bursting. She'd learned the day before that Aunt Frances had invited the Swearingens to spend the Fourth with all of them. And Truman was invited as well.

"The more the merrier," Aunt Frances had said.

Edie and Nell were thrilled at the prospect of spending the entire day with one another. And of course Lydia was happy to have Truman included.

After watching the festive downtown parade, complete with marching bands and decorative floats, the families gathered in the Allertons' backyard. The boys helped carry out tables and chairs and place them beneath the shade trees. Edie and Carl and Tim volunteered to accompany the Swearingens to their house to help carry food and more tables and chairs.

Tim was nearly as tall as Mr. Swearingen, who was a short, stout, studious-looking man with fair features and soft hands. The man didn't smile much.

Edie had been at Nell's house only a few times and didn't know Nell's parents very well; but as she observed them, she marveled that Nell was so outgoing and cheerful.

Nell's mother was a tall buxom woman with a very straight mouth. Her graying hair, which was pulled straight back into a chignon, made her face seem even more severe. Her tailored shirtwaist and long navy linen skirt were of few frills, unlike Edie's two aunts.

Mrs. Swearingen led the girls into the kitchen, where their arms were loaded with pans of fried chicken and dishes of cucumber salad and cole slaw. While Edie and Nell were laughing and talking, Mrs. Swearingen said little. Even though Edie was sure Nell's parents were kind, loving people, she was thankful that her own family members weren't quite that serious.

Tim and Carl helped Uncle Richard put out the wickets for games of croquet, and Nell and Edie kept watch over Harry and Adeline. Both girls were infatuated with the demure, quiet Addy. She was quite a contrast against the noisy, blustery, mischievous Harry. And while they would never fight over the little girl, both of them wanted to hold her.

Aromas of fried chicken and juicy corn on the cob filled the still summer air and mingled with the acrid smell of smoke from Carl's and Larry's firecrackers. It was a chore keeping Harry away from the dangerous explosives. He was such a curious little fellow.

The menfolk sat around talking, while the women filled the tables with endless varieties of scrumptious foods. Truman and Tim pulled up chairs and included themselves in the men's group. Edie could remember a time when Tim would have been off playing with Carl, but no more.

Aunt Esther was bright and vivacious and full of bubbly laughter. She and Aunt Frances hit it off famously with their similar vibrant personalities. Aunt Esther was much more outgoing than either Uncle Richard or Mama. Edie loved to hear Aunt Esther tell stories of their growing-up years, especially since Aunt Esther was the youngest in her family, just as Edie was in hers.

At last, all was in readiness. Blankets were spread in the shade in addition to the chairs that had been brought out, making room for everyone to have a place to sit. Uncle Richard prayed a blessing over the picnic dinner, and amid much talking and joking, they heaped their plates with food.

"I haven't had such a grand and glorious Fourth of July since I left Minneapolis," Uncle Erik commented, his smile beaming beneath the handlebar mustache. "I'm thankful that Esther and I could be a help to my aunt and uncle, but I'm even more thankful to be back home again."

He laughed and shook his head. "No more pigs to feed. Now that's enough to make a man shout for joy!"

Aunt Esther pointed to Mr. Benecroft's chicken pen. "And no more chickens, either, don't forget," she added.

"No more chickens, either," he agreed.

Since the women were still working to cut pies and fill glasses of lemonade, Edie and Nell attempted to help Harry and Addy with their plates. Addy kept her finger in her mouth, so it was difficult to know just what she did and didn't want. Harry, on the other hand, kept grabbing at the edge of the table and pulling at the tablecloth. Edie was sure he was going to tip something over on top of himself.

Gloria, having been through the line, was already seated on a blanket. Calling to her, Edie said, "Gloria, could you give us a hand with these little ones?"

To Edie's surprise, Gloria turned her back and acted as though she hadn't heard. Edie stared at her for a moment, wondering what was wrong. Gloria was always willing to help both Edie and Nell. But Edie shrugged it off. Perhaps her cousin was out of sorts about something that had happened between her and Larry.

Edie and Nell sat with the little ones on a blanket near where the men were gathered. As she and Nell helped to feed the little ones—and stuff themselves as well—they could listen to the talk. Edie was not surprised when it turned to the war.

Truman was telling of the first days of the Battle of Somme, which had begun on July 1. Some sixty thousand British soldiers had been slaughtered in a single day. "The Germans are dug in so tight that no amount of shelling can destroy their bunkers," he said.

Tim, who was fascinated with any and all machinery, talked about the new "land battleships" that the British had manufactured. "They're built all of metal and run on caterpillar treads but can carry machine guns," Tim explained. "Some people call it a tank. Inventions like these are what's needed on battlefields nowadays."

"More and bigger machines so more people can be killed," Uncle Richard said sadly. "It's fruitless. Hopeless. Insane." Waving an ear of half-eaten corn, he said, "I like what William Jennings Bryan says. He says that America is to be the supreme example of peace for all the world to look at and hope from."

"Those soft words are a pipe dream, Richard," Uncle Erik countered. "Good old Rough Rider Roosevelt is the one we should be listening to. Teddy isn't afraid to speak his mind clearly about Wilson's dallying. While 'Pussyfoot' Wilson is thinking things over, thousands of innocent civilians are being slaughtered each and every day."

Edie noticed that Papa didn't say much, but she knew his heart. He hoped that President Wilson would be re-elected, and he hoped America would never have to go to war.

Truman, as usual, was quite vocal. Mincing no words, he said, "There shouldn't be another moment wasted. Wilson should have declared war long ago. He should have done it the moment the *Lusitania* was sunk. If he had, the war would be over by now."

As she listened, Edie was amazed that both sides sounded right to her. How could that be? Truman's comments made her believe that American troops would make all the difference in winning the war. And yet she knew that meant Americans might have to die, and she certainly didn't want that, so peace seemed to be the better choice.

Papa then commented that the United States had no strong army. "The little run-in our troops had with Pancho Villa down in Mexico last March shows we're not as top-notch as we'd like to think we are."

Edie remembered that in geography class, Miss Hedley had told about the attack of Pancho Villa on a small town in New Mexico and how General "Black Jack" Pershing had rushed to the scene with detachments of U.S. fighting men. But nothing ever came of it. Papa's opinion about the whole incident was that no one was willing to admit that the Mexican *bandido* was too shrewd for the U.S. Army.

Uncle Erik followed up on Papa's comments. "We would

have taken that wily lizard easily enough if the War Department had accepted all the offers of civilian aeroplanes that came in. If war is declared with Germany," he went on, "thousands of young men will volunteer to serve and fight, just you wait and see."

"And I'll be one of the first!" Truman proclaimed proudly.

That was all Edie could bear. She hurried Nell to finish eating so they could play a game of croquet while the little ones were napping. She didn't want to hear another word about war.

The girls played against Carl and Larry, and the boys won two out of three games. But that was because they used the croquet mallets with such force. They loved knocking the girls' balls clear off the playing course.

That evening there were fireworks to set off—Roman candles, sparklers, pinwheels, and rockets. The orange and crimson explosions against the dark night sky made Edie wonder if that was what bombs looked like when they fell from the skies in France.

Aunt Esther wasted no time in getting involved with all the same clubs as Aunt Frances. She was as grateful as her husband to be back in the city once again. It was quickly established that Nell would help with the children because Addy would also be with them three afternoons a week. Nothing could have pleased Edie more. Now they were both mother's helpers. Aunt Esther brought Addy over to the Allertons', and the two mothers left from there.

The days were filled with laughter and fun and good times. Edie still had her work to do at home, because it was up to her to keep the house neat and clean and to prepare supper each evening. But her chores at home were easy to complete when she had so many good things to look forward to.

As Edie tended to the housework while the rest of the family was at work, Frosty kept her company. He jumped up on the beds as she straightened the covers and fluffed the pillows. He chased the broom as she swept out the kitchen, and he followed her every step as she dusted the parlor. When it was time for her to leave for the Allertons', Frosty curled up on a windowsill in the warm sunshine and fell fast asleep.

Edie used to wish their little house was as nice and well furnished as her aunt Frances's house. But Papa had told her a story about a cow who thought the grass was greener on the other side of the fence so she kept sticking her head through the fence. One day her head got caught in the twisted wire, and she couldn't get loose. Not only was she worse off than before, but she found the grass wasn't any better than her own. Edie tried to remember that story whenever she became envious of others.

Edie and Nell became a good team, keeping a close eye out for the little ones. Since they both loved fussing over and babying darling Addy, they found it was best to take turns with Harry, who was such a mischievous handful. Their plan worked perfectly. That is, they thought it was working perfectly until Gloria began to act strangely.

One afternoon they were playing with dolls and toys on a blanket in the backyard. It had grown stifling hot, so being beneath the shade trees was the best place to catch the slightest breeze. Down the street, Larry was playing baseball with a group of neighbor boys in a friend's yard.

Quiet little Addy had come onto the blanket, her finger in her mouth as usual. She reached down and picked up one of Gloria's dolls. Immediately Gloria grabbed it out of her hands.

"No, Adeline!" she snapped. "Play with your own dolls."

"Gloria," Edie scolded, "that's an unkind way to act to Addy. She won't hurt your doll."

"She might. She's only a baby." With that, Gloria put the doll in a little white wicker pram with wide metal tires. The pram looked just like one for a real baby, but it was for Gloria's dolls. Gloria had so many nice toys to play with.

Addy's wide eyes teared up, and her lip came out in a little pout. But in a moment she forgot the doll when she discovered the pretty pram. Toddling over to it, she gave it a push and was delighted when it rolled forward. Her dark eyes sparkled as she gave a big smile.

Again, Gloria snapped at her. "No, Adeline! That's my pram, and I'm taking my dolly for a walk."

"Stop being so selfish," Edie said to Gloria. "You know we always share when we're playing together. Nell and I play with your toys every day, and you've never fussed about it."

"That's different!" Gloria said. "You're not babies."

"That's unkind, Gloria," Edie said in her firmest voice. "If you don't share the toys, I'll have to tell your mama on you when she comes home."

"Go right ahead," Gloria said as she pushed her pram, carrying the doll back to the house. "See if I care. I don't care at all. Not one bit I don't."

When she was almost to the house, she called back over her shoulder, "Larry was right—you're not a very good mother's helper."

Edie looked over at Nell, but Nell just shrugged. "Maybe it's a stage she's going through," Nell suggested. "That's what Mama always says about me."

"I hope you're right."

Edie and Nell had brought out their tatting to work on, but not much tatting was done. Mostly they had to protect Addy from Harry. The little boy didn't know his own strength. Addy was always getting knocked down. "It's too bad Larry's not closer in age to Harry," Nell commented. "Harry needs another boy to roughhouse with."

They were so distracted, Edie hadn't even noticed that Gloria had been gone for a time. When she mentioned it, Nell said, "Perhaps she's taking a nap."

"Would you go inside and check on her?" Edie asked. "I'll stay here and watch the little ones."

Nell jumped up. "I'll bring the lemonade when I come back out."

"Great idea."

But when Nell returned she wasn't carrying the tray with the pitcher of lemonade. "Look at this, Edie." She knelt down on the blanket and handed Edie a piece of paper. "It's from Gloria."

In her childish scrawl, Gloria had written, *You like Addy better than me. Nobody likes me anymore. I'm going to run away.*

CHAPTER 10

Junior Red Cross Workers

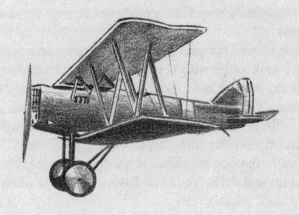

So that was it! "Oh, Nell, I've been a dunderhead," Edie said with a groan. "I should have seen what we were doing. Here we've been fussing over Addy, and it's made Gloria pea-green with envy."

"I think you're right. But what can we do?"

"There's only one thing we can do. She can't have gone far. Let's go find her and apologize."

"But what about Addy and Harry?"

"We could take them with us," Edie said.

"I have a better idea. I'll stay here, and you go to Gloria. I think she needs you."

Just then Larry came running up all out of breath. "What's Gloria doing walking in the next block all by herself? I thought you were supposed to be taking care of her," he said. "I knew you wouldn't be a very good mother's helper."

"Larry, stop saying that," Edie sputtered. "You've got Gloria saying it. Now you stay here and help with Harry, and I'll go get Gloria and bring her home."

Edie walked off briskly and just three blocks from the house caught sight of Gloria pushing her little pram down the sidewalk.

Edie slowed her pace and then sauntered up beside Gloria. "May I walk along with you?" she asked her younger cousin.

Gloria stopped and looked up at Edie with a heavy scowl on her face. "Go on back and play with Adeline and leave me alone." She resumed her walk, pushing the pram in front of her.

"But it's no fun without you there," Edie said. "No fun at all. You're the one who always has the best ideas about playing house and dolls. You even have good ideas when we play school. Nell said so."

Gloria stopped again. "Nell said so?"

"Uh huh. Nell likes you a lot."

Gloria started to smile, but then remembered and put her scowl back on. "Not as much as she likes Adeline. Everyone likes Adeline better than me."

Edie walked along beside Gloria for a few more steps. She needed to get Gloria back home before Aunt Frances returned. "You like Nell better than me," she said, "but I never minded that at all."

Surprise registered on Gloria's face. "Oh no, that's not true, Edie. I like you both the same."

"Really?"

"Really. Honest. Cross my heart."

"Well, I guess it's just that sometimes you *act* like you like her more than me."

"Maybe I do act that way," Gloria said, slowing her step. "But I don't mean it that way."

"I guess you can say that's also true about Nell and me. We may have acted like Addy was more special than you, but it's not true at all. We love you very much, and we miss you not being there."

Now the pram was stopped.

"We were about to have lemonade," Edie said. "You're probably thirsty from your long walk."

"I am thirsty," Gloria agreed. Her little face was flushed from the heat. Edie had never noticed before, but Gloria's face, with its fine features and fair complexion, was much like Addy's. The two cousins favored one another a great deal. She'd have to remember to fuss over Gloria more in the future.

"I'm thirsty, too. Let's walk back together. We'll have lemonade, and then we'll play school. Nell and I want you to be the teacher this time."

"Me? Truly?"

"Truly."

"We'd better hurry back then." And Gloria turned the pram around right there.

After that, Nell and Edie put their heads together and decided to ask Aunt Frances if they could do something special with Gloria and Larry and leave the little ones at home. They decided that the next Saturday, they would all go to a matinee at the Bijou Theater. Carl said a western was playing. Westerns, of course, were Carl's favorite movies. He dreamed of going out west one day and living in the wide open spaces. When he was younger, he talked about being a cowboy. Nowadays, he said he'd make his living taking landscape photographs for postcards.

Aunt Frances wasn't too keen on the flickers. Nor were Mama and Papa for that matter. But it was decided that a cowboy show couldn't hurt. Nell and Edie made sure that Gloria sat between them on the trolley as they rode from the Allertons' neighborhood to downtown. Larry and Carl sat in the seat right behind them. It was rather pleasant not to have to be constantly mindful of Harry and his antics. Gloria bounced happily in the seat, full of excitement. Edie glanced over at Nell and smiled. Their plan was working.

The dark interior of the theater was cooler than the bright hot street. Just as they located their seats in the semi-darkness, the light from the projection booth pierced through the dark theater and splashed a big white square on the screen. The pianist down front began to play dramatic music to accompany the moving pictures.

The newsreel appeared on the screen first. There were pictures of President Wilson and his wife walking along hand-in-hand in front of the White House. Words appeared on the screen, telling about his bid for re-election. From there the scene shifted to suffragettes who were picketing for the right to vote. A question came on the screen as to what Wilson planned to do about the women.

News of the war came next. The newsreel showed a British flying ace. The pilot was called an ace because he had shot down a certain number of German aeroplanes. The pilot's face was so young, almost as young-looking as Truman's. On his tight-fitting leather cap with earflaps were a pair of goggles. Around his neck was a snappy-looking white scarf. As he smiled into the camera, he pulled his goggles down over his eyes and climbed up into his plane, which was equipped with a machine gun.

"I'm going to fly a plane like that when I grow up," Larry whispered.

From the scene of the aeroplane taking off down a short runway, the film changed to a place in France. The words on the screen read, "Killer Huns Using Dreaded Gas." On the screen were a row of soldiers in filthy, tattered uniforms with their eyes wrapped in white bandages. Each man had his hand on the shoulder of the man in front as they stumbled along, being led by a sighted man. These soldiers had been temporarily blinded by an attack of poison gas from the enemy.

The awful sight made Gloria cover her eyes and begin to whimper. Edie put her arm around Gloria's shoulders to comfort her. She felt like crying herself. How could human beings do such horrid things to other human beings?

The cowboy show was almost ruined for Edie. How she wished they could watch the fun show without seeing the ghastly scenes from the newsreel. She didn't want to know the details of what was happening—especially not terrible things the Germans were doing.

She wondered if seeing such things made Nell feel differently toward her. Although Nell acted no different, how could Edie know what she was really thinking? Perhaps people were right in hating all Germans. If they shot poison gas at unsuspecting soldiers, perhaps they were truly as bad as people said they were.

When they arrived home from the moving picture show, Aunt Frances said she had a surprise for Nell and Edie. Edie was overjoyed. She needed something to make her forget the frightening war scenes.

"I've arranged for the two of you to join the Junior Red

Cross workers. Would you like that?"

"Would we ever!" Edie replied. How much better it would be to help out rather than just stare helplessly at the newsreels. "But I don't know what Mama would say. And wouldn't it interfere with my work for you?"

Aunt Frances laughed. "First of all, I've already asked Anna." Looking at Nell, she added, "And I've asked your mama as well. Both are agreeable. You'll work for three hours every Saturday morning. That won't interfere at all with your helping me."

Edie looked at Nell. Her friend's eyes were shining. If it were not for maintaining their ladylike appearance in front of Aunt Frances, they would have been jumping up and down and squealing.

"What will we be doing at the center?" Edie asked.

"Oh, there's ever so much work to do. That's why they're asking for more volunteers. They roll bandages, sew clothes, and knit stockings and sweaters."

Nell smiled. "Looks as though we'll be trading in our tatting hooks for knitting needles," she said.

CHAPTER 11
Truman's News

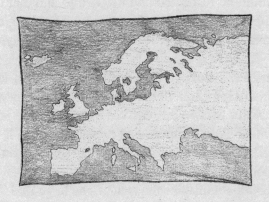

The Red Cross Center was located in a storefront building downtown. Edie decided to walk and save trolley-fare money. Nell, however, had farther to come, so Edie waited for her at the trolley stop at the corner of Washington and Second Avenue. The early morning downtown traffic was heavy with automobiles vying for positions among the slower horse-pulled drays and delivery wagons. She sat on a bench and watched well-dressed men on their way to their offices.

Mama had seemed pleased that Edie was going to do volunteer work. Mama's reaction surprised Edie because Mama was never one to get involved much. At least not like Aunt

Frances did. But of course working long hours at the freight company prevented Mama from having the freedom that Aunt Frances and Aunt Esther had. Sometimes in the evenings, Lydia would rub Mama's shoulders, which became tight and sore from sitting at her typewriting machine all day long.

Papa hated that Mama had to work, but his salary at the mill simply wasn't enough. Sometimes the mill owners would cut salaries with no warning at all. That's why Papa was such a strong supporter of the unions. Often he said that one day the unions would be respected and listened to and that the unions would help workers bargain for improved working conditions and reasonable salaries. How Edie wished that day were here now.

When Nell's trolley arrived, the girls walked together to the center, talking excitedly all the way. Aunt Frances had told them to ask for Mrs. Winifred Garland. "Winifred is in charge of the center," Aunt Frances had explained. "She'll show you around, give you your headdresses and smocks, and tell you what to do."

One could not mistake the center. The large Red Cross flags in the windows and a sign above the door proclaimed the work going on inside. The girls stepped in through the heavy front door to see a large room filled with women and girls all dressed in voluminous white smocks that covered their dresses. Their headdresses were made of a band with the red cross on the front, and a scarflike fabric that flowed out from the band. These too were all in white. Many of these volunteers, Edie knew, also gave unselfishly of their time to work with the suffrage movement in the city. Because of the war in Europe, they chose to direct their attention to a more desperate need than procuring the vote for women.

Rows and rows of tables were stacked high with piles of fabric. Some of the women were clustered about the tables cutting cloth into strips, while others worked at the knitting machines. Still others operated the hand-crank machines that worked to roll the bandages. Several sat in a circle off to the side knitting sweaters by hand.

Edie had heard Aunt Frances talk about this place many times. Now she could see for herself all the wonderful work that went on here. And better yet, now she would be a part.

Edie politely asked one of the ladies if they could see Mrs. Garland. "I'll get her," the lady answered. "I believe she's in the back. A new shipment of wool yarn has just come in."

Presently a plump, smiling lady came up to greet the girls. The scarf of her headdress was red rather than white. Perhaps that was because she was in charge, Edie thought.

"Welcome," she said in a cheery voice. "Which one of you is Mrs. Allerton's niece Edith?"

"Me," Edie said. "I mean, I am. And this is my friend Janelle Swearingen. But she goes by Nell. And you can call me Edie."

"Good to have you with us, Nell, Edie. Frances tells me you two are very good workers. As you can see, that's what's needed here. In spite of all we provide from this center, it's a drop in the bucket to what is needed. Thousands of men are wounded in France every day, yet there are never enough bandages nor enough bedclothes for the hospitals."

Edie had never thought about the need for bedclothes. But then she'd never thought of thousands of hospital beds either.

Mrs. Garland went on to explain to them that the Minneapolis Suffrage Association had begun a fund-raising campaign in order to open their own hospital in France.

"It will be completely staffed by women," she told them. "And the French government is totally in favor of the idea."

She leaned closer and smiled as though she were sharing a secret. "It seems the French have no prejudice against women surgeons and nurses such as we experience here in America."

Her comment reminded Edie of Lydia, who was forever saying that women could do anything men could do, and sometimes do it better.

After Mrs. Garland showed them around, introduced them to several of the workers, and explained the various jobs, she took them to the back to fetch their headdresses.

"There's a place where you may hang up your hats," Mrs. Garland said, "and a mirror over here." After their hats were removed, Mrs. Garland showed them how to fasten the bands in the back, and she helped to fluff and straighten the scarves. "We haven't enough smocks just now, but more are being made. Perhaps in a week or two we'll have smocks for you as well."

Edie gazed at her reflection. How trim and clean the white headdress looked; how important it made her feel. She reached up to straighten the scarf. Just then Nell leaned closer. "It's almost like a wedding veil," she whispered.

"You're right," Edie whispered back. "It is."

Mrs. Garland directed them to a table where workers were cutting cloth strips. This was where they were to begin. She showed them the markers on the edges of the table that helped them to gauge the size of the strips. "They don't have to be exact," she said, "but we do want them to be generally the same width."

So for three hours, they cut and cut and cut. Little prickles of pain were shooting up Edie's back and neck long before the time was over. And where the scissors had rubbed on her thumb, a red raw blister had appeared.

"It's not easy work," said one of the ladies when she

noticed Edie rubbing her neck. "But when we think of those who are suffering in the trenches over there in France, our pain seems like nothing at all."

Edie wasn't sure she could make that thinking work. Her shoulders were screaming. She was awfully glad when their three hours were up and it was time to go.

Now with her Saturday mornings taken, Edie was busier than ever, and the summer days were speeding by much too quickly. While she was pleased to be a help, she also wanted to reach out and grab hold of the sweet leisurely warm days and force them to linger longer. On August 20 she would turn twelve years old, and she could hardly wait. What an exciting day that would be.

Throughout the summer, Truman and Carl had been experimenting together with night photography. In the evenings they loaded their cameras and equipment and took the trolley downtown, where they photographed the glittering lights of the signs, the street lamps, and the moving automobiles.

Tim teased them about it. "Who wants to look at pictures of lights?" he asked.

But Truman saw photography as much more than just snapping pictures for the family photo album. "I believe it can become an art form," he would say. "The more we learn about shades of lighting and techniques with our cameras, the more we can create and control the illusions we wish to make."

Edie could tell that Carl hung on every word. While Truman was older even than Timothy, still it was the love of photography that had cemented the relationship between him and young Carl.

They were an odd pair, since Truman was vocal and outspoken while Carl was quiet and reserved. In spite of their differences both in personality and age, they made a good team.

"Before you know it," Truman said to Carl once, "you'll be selling your photographs to fine magazines like *National Geographic*."

When Truman said such things, Edie wondered why he never included himself. Surely he'd be accomplishing such feats before Carl ever did. Truman had offered to get Carl a job inside the newspaper office being a runner for the newsroom, but Carl had turned it down.

"The daily headlines are as close to the news as I care to get," he told Truman.

Edie wasn't sure that was the complete truth, because Carl read the papers from cover to cover, not just the headlines. And he was intensely interested in the news. She thought it was because Carl preferred to be alone. On his paper route, he was in charge and he could be by himself. As a news runner in the office, he would have to answer to many people.

Truman had become a regular presence at the Schmidt household, a presence with whom everyone seemed comfortable. Edie was sure he was there for more than just photography. Edie thought it would be terribly romantic if Truman would ask Papa to allow Lydia to go out with him. But it never happened.

One night she found out why. Truman had things on his mind other than Lydia or photography. As usual, he and Carl had been working in the shed. When supper was ready, there was a place set for Truman. The summer evening was quite warm, so Edie had decided to have cold sliced beef tongue for supper. All the windows were open to let in what little breeze there was, and she didn't want to have to fire up the gas stove if she could help it. The produce bins in the markets were overflowing with good things now that summer was in full swing, so it was easy to have cold fruits and vegetables at every meal.

Later she would remember every detail of how the supper

went. How good everything tasted, and how pleasant it was to have the family gathered together sharing things that had happened during the day. Lydia always had funny stories about customers she encountered while measuring and cutting fabrics in Woolworth's bargain basement. Tim told of new things he was learning at the offices of W & S Engineering. This fall would begin Tim's senior year at Central High School, and already he was planning how he could work his way through college. He had definite plans about becoming an engineer.

Truman generally joined right in all the noisy talk—often being the most vocal of all. But tonight Edie noticed he was quieter than usual.

Early that morning she had prepared vanilla egg custard. She'd baked it in Mama's little Pyrex custard bowls and then set them on a tray in the icebox. Of course she made sure there was an extra one just in case Truman might be there.

When they'd finished supper, she went to the icebox to retrieve the tray and was putting a bowl at each place when Truman cleared his throat. "I have something I'd like to say," he said.

Edie clutched the tray more tightly. This was it! He was finally getting up the nerve to ask to take Lydia out.

"What is it, Truman?" Papa asked in his kindest voice. Perhaps Papa was thinking the same thing Edie was thinking.

"I will be leaving Minneapolis on the train this Saturday. I've joined the American Field Ambulance in France."

Lydia's hand flew to her mouth to stifle an audible gasp.

The tray slipped from Edie's hand and hit the floor with a horrific clatter.

CHAPTER 12

Two Good-byes

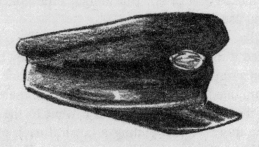

Truman leaped to his feet. "Here, Edie. Let me help you."

"No, that's all right. I have it." Strangely, the last custard bowl—which was hers—had landed upright. Not a bit was spilled. Frosty rubbed up against her as she retrieved the bowl and the tray.

Truman's words were too unbelievable to comprehend. There was silence until Edie returned to her place. Papa spoke first. "You have thought this through clearly, ja?" Papa always slipped into German when he was upset.

"Yes, sir, I have. I've thought it through a great deal."

Carl's face was pale and drawn. "You can't go, Truman," his voice croaked. "You just can't."

"This is something I feel I have to do. It's a place where I can serve until President Wilson finally decides to let us fight."

"We'll miss you," Mama said softly. She too had become quite attached to this fine young man.

"I know. I'll miss all of you, too." He turned to look at Lydia. "I'll miss all of you very much. I hope you'll write to me."

The rest of the evening was a blur. Nothing was the same. Before that night, the faces in France were dim and gray. No one was familiar in any way. But now there would be a face in France that Edie knew. Suddenly the war didn't seem so far away anymore.

Perhaps this was why Truman never included himself in the plans he'd spoken of with Carl. He never included himself because all along he'd planned on going away.

That night as she and Lydia prepared for bed, Lydia was quiet and said nothing. Edie wanted to get her to talk, but she didn't know how. And nothing she could say would make any difference anyway. Lydia had continually said she didn't care all that much about Truman. But now she might never get the chance to find out for sure exactly how she did feel. How unfair that was.

Late into the night, Edie was awakened by a sound beside her. A little sniffle, then another. Lydia's weeping was muffled in her pillow but still very loud in the quiet room.

Edie longed to comfort Lydia, but what could she do? Her feelings shifted from sadness for Lydia to smoldering anger against Truman. How could he do this to them after all they'd done for him? How dare he just up and leave them like that? As she struggled to go back to sleep, Edie decided that Truman Vaught was just an ungrateful, horrible young man!

Truman asked that only Lydia come to the train station to

see him off on Saturday morning, and he would say good-bye to the rest of the family on Friday evening. Edie was surprised that Papa would allow Lydia to go to the station by herself, but he did.

Friday night turned out to be a somber occasion. After supper, Truman asked Mama to get out their old family album. He wanted to look at the pictures of the family as they were growing up. He thanked Mama and Papa for letting him be a part of their family. His own family was quite small, consisting only of him and his widowed mama, and he'd relished the times with all the Schmidts.

The hour grew late, and when it was time for him to go, Truman shook hands with each of them. As he did, Frosty came and rubbed back and forth against Truman's legs. Truman reached down to pet the cat. "I'll even miss you, Frosty," he said.

To Carl, he said, "I expect you to send me photographs as well as letters. I want to know how you're progressing."

Carl could only nod. Edie didn't look over at Carl. She didn't have to. She knew his eyes were tear-filled. All of their eyes were tear-filled. After Truman had said good-bye to each one, they walked out onto the front porch in the still summer evening. The cicadas were singing their summer concert in the trees along the street. An old Model T rumbled by. Horns honked in the distance and the trolley bell clanged its warning. Somewhere a Victrola was playing the song "I Didn't Raise My Boy to Be a Soldier."

"Good-bye," Truman called out to them as he walked away. "Write to me. I'll be back. I promise. I'll be back." To Lydia, he said, "I'll see you in the morning at the train station."

Then he walked away. Just like that he was gone. Lydia turned and ran into the house and up the stairs, slamming the door to their room. Carl disappeared into his darkroom.

Edie and Mama cleaned up the kitchen. Mama washed the dishes, and Edie wiped each one dry and put them away. Neither of them said a word about Truman. It was just too painful to talk about.

As far as Edie was concerned, Truman had ruined the entire summer. Carl moped around, and so did Lydia. Papa and Tim attempted to cheer them up, but it did little good. And here Edie's birthday was just around the corner. She'd been secretly hoping that Mama and Lydia would buy new dress fabric for her birthday. Fabric to make into new school dresses. But with Lydia in the frame of mind she was in, how would she ever think to look for fabric for Edie?

Edie had to admit, though, that even she missed Truman. He'd spent so much time with them, he'd truly become part of the family. She wondered what had happened at the train station that Saturday. Had he pledged his love to Lydia? Had he kissed her good-bye? Edie might never know because Lydia said nothing.

The next time Edie and Nell were together, she told her friend all about Truman's departure.

"That's the saddest thing I've ever heard of," Nell said. She got all teary in spite of the fact that she'd barely known Truman.

By the first of August, the heat of summer was pressing down in full force. Edie found herself getting snippy with the children. Gloria and Larry were short tempered, and Harry was constantly making Addy cry about something or other. Even good-natured Aunt Frances admitted the heat was getting to her.

On Friday, the day before Edie's twelfth birthday, she

arrived at Aunt Frances's house just after lunch as usual. Aunt Frances and Aunt Esther were ready to leave to go to a meeting.

They were standing in the front hallway looking somewhat perplexed.

After greeting Edie, Aunt Esther said to Aunt Frances, "I think it's too much to ask of her."

"I agree it would be a handful," said Aunt Frances.

"What would be a handful?" Edie asked. "And where's Nell?" Nell was always there when Edie arrived.

"She's not coming today." Aunt Frances stood with her gloves dangling in her hands. "And I think it would be too much to ask you to handle all four children by yourself."

"Nell's not coming? Is she sick?"

"Now, Frances," Aunt Esther put in, "Mrs. Swearingen said she might let Nell come over later."

"You're right. She did say that," Aunt Frances answered.

Edie was getting frustrated. "What's going on? What's wrong with Nell?"

"Oh dear, Edie. I'm sorry," Aunt Frances said. "It's her brother."

"Devlin? Is Devlin hurt?"

"No. Not yet anyway. He telephoned to tell them he's applied to the Recruiting Service Customs House in Boston to join the merchant marines."

Edie stood frozen. Devlin going away to sea. How perfectly dreadful. Poor Nell. "I need to go to her. I need to be with Nell."

Aunt Esther put her hand on Edie's shoulder. "Of course you do, dear. And we should be thinking of Mrs. Swearingen as well. What terrible news this is for the entire family. Frances, you telephone the ladies and tell them we can't make the suffrage meeting today." She waved at her face with her gloves. "Truth be told, I didn't want to put these gloves on in this heat anyway."

Aunt Frances smiled. "You're right." To Edie she said, "You run on over there and be with Nell. We'll fix something and bring it to Mrs. Swearingen later on."

At the Swearingens' house, the housekeeper answered the door and led Edie to the front parlor. Mrs. Swearingen and Nell were seated on the small settee by the bay windows. Edie could tell both had been crying.

She went over to Nell, put her arms about her, and said, "Aunt Frances told me about Devlin. I'm so sorry, Nell."

"Thank you, Edie. Thank you for coming," Nell said. "Our Devlin is such an adventurer. He never did like school—not one bit."

"We should have guessed he'd do something like this," her mother put in, dabbing at her eyes with a lace hankie. "He told me he walked by the Shipping Board Recruiting Office nearly every day. I suppose being in such close proximity to the sea and seeing the brightly colored posters in the recruiting office window were too much for him to resist."

Mrs. Swearingen stood to her feet. In spite of the stifling heat, apart from her red eyes, she appeared fresh and cool in her tailored summer dress. "I suppose it's silly of us to be sitting here like this, Janelle dear. Things must be done to ready the place for his visit."

"He's coming home for two days to tell us good-bye," Nell said to Edie. As she said the words she began to cry again. Edie sat down beside her and held her.

"I'm sorry not to be able to help you at the Allertons'," Nell added, sniffing loudly. Mrs. Swearingen handed her a clean handkerchief.

"Aunt Frances and Aunt Esther decided to stay home from

their meeting," Edie said. "So there's nothing to be sorry about."

"Oh dear. And all because of me."

"It's nothing, Nell. We understand. There'll still be many more days this summer."

Nell nodded. But both of them knew the fun had gone out of what was left of summer.

Later Edie went back to Aunt Frances's house and helped keep the children out from underfoot while the two women baked a Lady Baltimore cake to take to the Swearingens.

Nell was supposed to come to the Allertons' on Saturday evening for Edie's birthday supper, but she declined, saying she'd better stay with her mama as much as possible. Edie was crestfallen. There was a lovely birthday cake that Mama had made and nice gifts from everyone. But it wasn't near as much fun without Nell there.

Lydia had fooled Edie by purchasing three new school dresses for her, which she'd found on the sale rack at Woolworth's. While Edie was thrilled to have real store-bought dresses, she'd been looking forward to sewing with Lydia. But she could tell Lydia simply wasn't in the mood to sew and talk and laugh like they'd done so many times before.

Devlin arrived back home the week after Edie's birthday. All the neighbors convened at the Swearingens', and of course the Schmidts were invited as well. Devlin was a happy-go-lucky kind of guy with a sharp wit and keen sense of humor. Edie was sure he must have been the heartthrob of his college campus with his dark wavy hair and handsome square jaw.

He explained to the guests at the lovely sit-down dinner that he was scheduled to report to the training ship called the *Meade* in Boston Harbor. There he would receive his uniform and equipment and a month of shore training. "I'll learn the use of the compass and the handling and splicing of ropes just as I did in Boy Scouts," he joked. "After my training, I'll be considered a naval apprentice and will have earned a berth on a regular merchant ship. Then off I go." He punctuated the words with a wave in the air of his water glass.

"Or *down* you go," Edie wanted to add, but she said nothing. After all, she knew the numbers of ships that were being sunk by the German U-boats. Ships were being destroyed faster than they could be manufactured. Carl had told her so.

In spite of the fact that he was leaving them, Devlin kept the guests chuckling and laughing throughout the formal mealtime. Even his tight-lipped mother looked more relaxed. He seemed to be the only person who could make Mrs. Swearingen smile.

But Devlin could turn serious as well, and when he was serious he sounded much like Truman Vaught. "The merchant ships are desperately in need of manpower," he told his small audience. "What good is it for us to increase production of goods here in the States if there's no way to get those goods into the hands of the Allies?"

"But Devlin," his father countered, "that's none of our concern."

"Now, Father," Devlin said with a twinkle in his eye. "You're sounding like our languishing president. He doesn't think it's our concern even when those filthy Huns sink our ships and kill Americans." Turning to Papa, he quickly added, "No offense, Mr. Schmidt."

"None taken," Papa said in his kindest voice.

And so, just as with every other time when the men gathered, the discussion turned to whether America should or should not be a part of the conflict. Only now the discussion was a little different. Edie could see that many men were deciding to join in the fray no matter what President Wilson said.

Carl had read in the paper that scores of college students were dropping out of school and joining the American Field Ambulance just as Truman had. This in spite of the fact that some ambulance drivers had been killed by German artillery fire on their dash from the front to the Paris hospitals. These daring young men were speaking with their actions, while the American government spoke with inaction.

After dinner, Devlin called Nell over to where he was sitting. Pulling a tiny package from his pocket, he said, "Here little pint-pot, I have something for you to remember me by after I'm gone."

As Edie watched Nell open the package, she wondered what she would feel like if it were her beloved Timothy who was leaving to go out on the high seas where German U-boats were sinking everything in sight. She couldn't even bear the thought.

Opening a velvet box, Nell gasped as she lifted out an exquisite silver thimble. "Oh, Devlin. It's so beautiful."

"Just like you are, sweetie," he said. "Now look inside."

Turning up the thimble to the light, she read, " 'Love to Sis from Devlin, 1916.' " She threw her arms around his neck. "I'll cherish this forever, Devlin. I love you so much."

Edie's throat was tight and her eyes hot. Beside her, Lydia was crying. This was like saying good-bye to Truman all over again.

CHAPTER 13

Letters from the Front

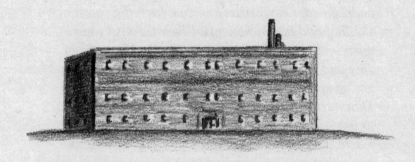

After Devlin went away, Nell was different. It wasn't anything that Edie could point out exactly. It was more like a sense—a feeling. Edie wondered if Nell was thinking more and more about the role the Germans were playing in the mammoth war. It was certain she was thinking of the terrible danger her brother would be in every day he was at sea.

Just before school began in September, a letter arrived from Truman. The Schmidt family gathered around in the parlor after dinner, and Papa asked Lydia if she wanted to read it aloud. She said she didn't think she could. Carl couldn't either.

In the end it was Tim who took the letter and began to read Truman's words.

First he described the city of Paris, calling it "something more beautiful than anything we have in the good old United States. The ancient buildings and monuments and cathedrals are magnificent beyond belief."

From there he went on to tell about the terrible battlefields:

It is like nothing you could ever imagine in your most vile nightmares. These soldiers are weary and bedraggled, nearly driven insane from the constant shelling and bombardments. When the heavy guns open up it's like the finale of a hundred Fourths of July and worse. First a barrage comes, then soldiers go "over the top" to begin hand-to-hand fighting. That means they leave the protection of their trenches to begin a terrifying run through "no man's land" where there are no trees and no foliage of any kind, but rather mud and barbed wire.

Mama shook her head. "If only he'd listened to us," she said. "Then he wouldn't be in the midst of all that terror and grief."

"But he feels he's doing what's right," Lydia answered. Tim continued:

At first when I saw all the dead bodies, I became violently ill. Some are left in the open air for so long before burial they are like bloated scarecrows. Some were buried in long pits and piled on top of each other like so many cigars in a box. The lines of fresh earth were so long, one could mistake them for more trenches. After a time, the corpses become just like the rest of the waste here—like the shattered walls, like the uprooted trees, like the fields desecrated by shells. Then it doesn't bother me so much.

Tim paused a moment. Even he was having difficulty with these gruesome facts. Swallowing hard, he continued.

There are many fellows my age here from the States. We all stay in an old hotel near the hospital. We save many many lives by our work with the Field Ambulance. One of my fellow ambulance drivers quoted me this poem:

Five hundred miles of Germans
  Five hundred miles of French,
And English, Scotch and Irish men
  All fighting for a trench;
And when the trench is taken
  And many thousand slain,
The losers, with more slaughter,
  Retake the trench again.

This is exactly how futile it all seems. I'm privileged to be a part of helping the proud French and the plucky Brits who are fighting so hard. And I still believe with all my heart that if Wilson would allow us to do so, we Yanks could turn the tide in a matter of days.

At the bottom of the letter was a note to Lydia saying a personal letter for her was coming soon.

The anger Edie felt against Truman once again rose inside of her. Not only had he made the war closer, now he had brought it into the very confines of their quiet parlor. How she wished they'd never met Truman in the first place.

Even though Edie's fifth-grade year hadn't been her happiest, still it had ended on a happy note, what with her winning the spelling bee and all. But she was soon to learn that the unpleasantness in fifth grade was mild compared to the opening days of sixth grade.

To start off, Papa came home saying he had been elected president of the local mill workers union. Whereas before he'd been an officer, now he was the leader and spokesman for the entire local union. Each family member knew what that meant. Now Papa would be more visible than ever. Mama told him she was proud of his accomplishment. Tim said the same thing. Edie, too, was proud of the stand her papa was taking, but at the same time, she felt the old familiar brassy taste of fear in her mouth.

The very night following the election, their telephone rang in the wee hours of the morning. Edie could hear Papa moving through the hallway to the kitchen to answer it. But after he said "Hello," there was no more talking. She heard him replace the receiver and walk back to the bedroom. About thirty minutes later it happened again.

"Stupid pranksters," Lydia whispered out loud into the darkness. Edie didn't answer. She just lay there hoping the phone calls were the worst that would happen.

When it happened the third time, the telephone rang and rang and rang. Papa was attempting to ignore it. But it never stopped ringing until he made his way to the kitchen to answer it once more. This time, she heard him say something more than just a hello, but the words were muffled. Edie was glad she could not hear the words. She didn't want to know what he said anyway. All she wanted to do was go back to sleep and pretend it was all a dream.

Papa looked more weary than usual the next morning. Even though everyone in the family had heard the prank calls, they were never mentioned.

After school started, Edie and Nell continued to volunteer at the Red Cross Center on Saturdays. Now when they arrived, they not only put on their headdresses but also their starched white smocks. Since their first days as volunteers, they'd been given several jobs to do in addition to cutting strips of cloth for bandages. Sometimes they hemmed sheets and pillow cases. When they did, Nell always pulled from her pocket her special silver thimble and wore it proudly. All the ladies fussed over it, and that gave Nell the opportunity to brag about her brave brother who was in the merchant marines.

While Edie couldn't help her aunts as often as in the summer, still she was there on Saturday afternoons. In fact, it was a Saturday afternoon in September when Nell received her first letter from Devlin, and she shared it with Edie. In his letter, he made crude jokes about Germans, but Edie acted as though it didn't bother her in the least. The important thing was that he was safe and that Nell was pleased to have a letter from him.

Their sixth-grade teacher, Mrs. Corbitt, seated her students in alphabetical order just as Miss Hedley had the year before. That meant that once again Sarah sat across from Nell, and both of them sat just behind Edie.

As usual Nell and Edie met at the schoolyard gate first thing each morning. Knowing that Nell was burdened with worry about Devlin, Edie racked her brain each morning to think of something cheerful and uplifting to say. Sometimes it would be a funny poem. Sometimes a Scripture verse she'd read. And she always reminded Nell that her family prayed for Devlin's safety each evening, just as they prayed for Truman's.

One day as she walked to school, Edie thought about her favorite hymn, "A Mighty Fortress Is Our God," and the Scripture it was taken from, Psalm 18. Both the hymn and the Scripture buoyed her faith whenever she was troubled and afraid.

When she arrived at school, she shared her thoughts with Nell. "When you write to Devlin, perhaps you can share the words of Martin Luther's hymn and remind him that God can be his mighty fortress."

"What a good idea," Nell said. "I hadn't thought about sharing a Scripture."

"Papa showed me that there are many verses that say God is our fortress, but my favorite is Psalm 18:2. Look what it says."

She handed Nell a card on which she'd written out the verse in her best penmanship. "Read it," she said.

"The Lord is my rock," Nell read aloud, "and my fortress, and my deliverer; my God, my strength, in whom I will trust; my buckler, and the horn of my salvation, and my high tower."

Looking up from the card, Nell said, "Thank you, Edie. It even helps *me* to feel better knowing that God can be Devlin's fortress and his high tower."

"Then it'll surely make him feel better, too. Don't you think?"

"It takes a long time for letters to get to him," she reminded Edie. "He's so far away from us. But I'll send it anyway. And I'll do it the very next time I write."

Nell's reply made Edie feel better. She so wanted to be an

encouragement. However, that same morning, before the first bell rang, Sarah Whalen and several other girls came over to where Edie and Nell were sitting on the jungle gym talking. This was the first time Sarah had ever come up to them. Usually she acted as though they didn't exist.

Ignoring Edie, she spoke right to Nell and said, "Janelle Swearingen, I can't believe you're still spending time with a traitor."

Nell squinted up her pretty brown eyes and stared right back at Sarah. "Edie is no traitor, and you know it, Sarah. Now stop talking like that."

"Oh, yes she is. During this time when all factories and businesses are working to aid the Allies, anyone who's part of the union is a traitor to the cause."

"That's right," put in another girl named Lorraine Jenner. "And Edie's father isn't just a member of a union, he's the *president*." Her face reflected her distaste as she said the word.

"And my father," Sarah went on, "says that any employee in his shoe factory who even thinks of joining a union will be dismissed on the spot."

"Well, your father's shoe factory is not the same as a flour mill," Nell said.

"It's all the same thing," Sarah insisted. "Union members are slackers who want to cause trouble and avoid work. And besides that, my father says it's those Huns who are behind most of the union movements. And that's exactly what Hans Schmidt is—a slacker, a troublemaker, and a dirty Hun."

"Come on, Edie," Nell said, gently taking Edie's trembling hand. "Let's go on inside."

But Sarah wasn't through. Stepping in front of Nell, she added, "Just remember, Janelle, if you continue to keep company with the daughter of a German troublemaker, everyone will think you're a traitor as well."

Edie felt Nell's grip on her hand tighten. Something deep inside Edie told her that Sarah's poison words had at last hit home.

CHAPTER 14

New Volunteers at the Center

Once Devlin had completed his month of naval training, his letters to Nell sported strange-looking foreign stamps from various countries. Nell read nearly every letter aloud to Edie.

A tinge of coolness was in the air and the aroma of burning leaves wafted over from a neighbor's backyard. Edie pulled her wool sweater more tightly around her as she and Nell sat on the Allertons' porch on an October afternoon reading yet another of Devlin's letters.

In the time that he'd been aboard the *St. Louis* as an active merchant marine, Devlin had crossed the Atlantic twice. While he had gone ashore at many of the stops, he said none of the crew were given shore leave in France.

"But we could hear the exploding shells into the night," he wrote in one letter. He also told of seeing the periscopes of U-boats out in open waters and described narrow escapes from the deadly torpedoes.

The letter Nell was reading this day told about some of his shipmates:

They come from all over the United States, from Maine to California. Good fellows they are who would give you the shirts right off their backs. Most are as anxious as I am for the U.S. to get into this war and get it over with. How I wish our ship were armed with some of those big guns. Then we'd show the enemy a thing or two.

"That's the way Truman talks in his letters," Edie told Nell. "Even though he sees how terrible the war is, he still feels we should be helping the British and the French."

Nell nodded, then continued reading:

On this trip we have a German boy onboard. Can you imagine anything so crazy? His name is Wilmott Achleitner. He's from Baltimore. He comes and goes about the ship and does his work, but hardly anyone talks to him. Some of the shipmates have nicknamed him Kaiser. Everyone watches him closely.

I suppose he's a good enough fellow all right. But after what we've seen of the wanton destruction in Europe, particularly the bomb raids in London, how could we ever trust him? I'm surprised they even allowed him to be on the crew.

Nell continued reading to the end of the letter, but Edie had stopped listening. Her friend seemed to have no idea how deeply those words from Devlin had cut into Edie's heart. For the life of her, she could not understand how a person's national allegiance could be determined by their name. This boy named Wilmott Achleitner might be as opposed to the German atrocities as Papa was. Who was to know?

President Wilson had conducted his entire presidential campaign on the slogan "He Kept Us Out of War." Papa liked the sound of that. Still, Papa said he wasn't sure anyone could continue to keep Americans out of the war. He was disturbed that the subject of the war was barely discussed at the Republican convention. All they had done was put their one candidate on the ticket, Charles Evans Hughes.

"How can they be so indifferent to such a crisis?" Papa had said at the time.

Edie wondered at what point the war had become a crisis to Papa. For a long time, he, too, had acted as though it didn't exist.

Election day arrived on November 7 that fall. It was a gray, drizzly type of early winter day. Papa was let off work early in order to cast his vote. Edie was scheduled to go straight to Aunt Frances's house after school. Edie's two activist aunts were joining crowds of suffragettes who were stationed outside the polling places, holding signs that demanded that women be allowed to vote. Lydia wanted very much to join the demonstrations, but she wasn't able to get off work.

In spite of being soaked to the skin and thoroughly chilled, Aunt Frances was jubilant when she returned home. "One day, Edie," she said, "all this demonstrating will be over. Mark my word. One day all women will be voting."

As confusing as everything seemed to be, Edie wasn't sure she even wanted to vote. How was a person to know what was right? Or who was right? Even though President Wilson said he was neutral, one editorial in the newspaper—which Carl had read aloud to the family one evening—stated that if Wilson truly were neutral, America wouldn't be sending tons of supplies to the Allies. That's how confusing it all was!

The morning after the election, Carl came home from his paper route carrying a copy of the *Tribune* with the bold banner headline: *HUGHES ELECTED IN CLOSE CONTEST?*

Carl told the story of how the presses had to be stopped and the question mark inserted. Newsmen all over the country had assumed that since the East Coast states voted for Hughes, the election had been decided. But that was not the case. Late returns from the West began to arrive, and they were solidly for Wilson.

The morning after the election, no one knew who was to be president! It wasn't until Thursday that word came that Wilson had actually won. The Western states successfully carried him over the top.

A letter arrived from Truman a couple weeks later stating that it really didn't matter to him who was president. "Just as long as the U.S. continues to give the Allies the support and materials that have already been afforded to them," he wrote. "Every type of supply is desperately needed."

Truman's descriptions of the homeless, hungry civilians—especially the children—broke their hearts. "Entire French villages have been completely destroyed," one letter informed them, "and the refugees can do nothing but stream into Paris and struggle to find food and shelter in order to survive."

Edie was glad she was helping at least a little bit by spending her Saturday mornings at the Red Cross Center.

Truman also wrote to the Schmidt family about the Battle of Verdun. It had been dragging on for months on end. He'd been told that the Germans had lost one hundred thousand men in just four days:

> *It's as though the Kaiser's only battle plan is to keep throwing men into the line of fire until more of the Allies die than Germans. It's such an insane way to fight a war. If only the Yanks were here.*

Nearly every letter ended that way. Truman had almost made a believer out of Edie. She wished something would happen to end the war quickly, even if it meant Americans having to fight. But then she thought of the possibility of Tim going off to war, and she changed her mind again.

One chilly Saturday morning, Aunt Frances was kind enough to drive by and pick Edie up to take her to the Red Cross Center. Aunt Frances had telephoned Edie on Friday evening, saying she was taking the children downtown shopping, and Uncle Richard had let her take the Hupmobile.

"I'll bring Nell as well," she added, "so she needn't take the trolley. It'll be on my way and won't be any trouble at all."

The Allertons' Hupmobile had a heater that made the car as cozy as a little cottage. As usual, Harry was clutching his teddy. "The two are inseparable," his mother quipped. "It makes me wonder if he'll be carrying it off to school with him in a few years."

Harry sat beside Edie and showed her the hole in its back. "Teddy has hole," he'd say, poking his finger into the opening to demonstrate.

"I do believe teddy has had a hole for a very long time, Harry," Edie said.

"I've sewed it up several times," Aunt Frances said. "But he works his finger in through the stitches. I think he prefers the hole."

"Maybe he likes the feel of the stuffing," Edie suggested.

"Could be," Aunt Frances said as she pulled to a stop in front of the center. "I'll be by to pick you up at noon. I need to talk to Mrs. Garland about other matters anyway. See you then."

The girls thanked her as they stepped down out of the warm automobile into the cold November air. A sharp wind was whipping around the tall buildings and blowing up bits of trash and dirt, making Edie and Nell hurry inside even faster.

The Red Cross Center was such a friendly place. In spite of the hard work, Edie relished being there each week. As they entered, they were met with cheery greetings from the other workers. Some volunteers began the work and then quit, but most of the women and girls were committed and dedicated. They came day after day, week after week.

Edie had heard Mrs. Garland talking about opening yet another center since this one was becoming so crowded. The scores of volunteers worked elbow-to-elbow with one another.

The girls hurried into the back, hung up their wraps, and slipped into their white headdresses and clean smocks. Today, Edie was to learn to operate the knitting machine. Next Saturday would be Nell's turn to learn. Mrs. Garland was keen on having the junior members learn everything and not just be stuck with the menial tasks.

As another worker demonstrated to Edie how to thread the knitting machine, the front door opened with a strong gust of cold wind. In walked Sarah Whalen, followed by her friend Lorraine. Sarah stood and scanned the room a moment. When she caught Nell's eye, she smiled and gave a little wave. Lorraine did the same.

Edie felt a sour taste rise up in her throat.

CHAPTER 15
Lost Thimble

"No dear," said the lady who was teaching her the knitting machine, "not like that. Like this." She took the yarn from Edie's fingers and again showed her how to thread it through the various hooks and holders. But all Edie could think of was the presence of Sarah Whalen in that room.

Mrs. Garland came up and greeted the newcomers just as sweetly as she had greeted Nell and Edie last summer when they first started. And why not? She needed every extra pair of hands that might be available.

There were no smocks available for the two newcomers, nor

extra headdresses. Edie was secretly glad. As Mrs. Garland talked to the girls and showed them around, Sarah pointed to Nell—probably telling Mrs. Garland that she knew Nell.

When Sarah and Lorraine were put to work, Edie wasn't surprised that they were seated at the table with Nell. She tried to sneak furtive glances in their direction. Each time she did, the three of them were chatting like long-lost friends. And each time she looked up, the knitting machine knotted, and she'd have to stop and fix it.

Edie was relieved when at last Aunt Frances came in with the children to take them home. Harry came running over to her, swinging teddy with every step. "Edie, Edie," he said, bouncing up to give her a big hug.

Aunt Frances went into the back to talk with Mrs. Garland, while Nell and Edie removed their smocks and put their warm coats back on. Edie said nothing to Nell about Sarah and Lorraine. What was there to say? She certainly couldn't stop people from volunteering at the center, and she couldn't stop Nell from talking to whomever she wished.

When they were all ready to leave, Harry was on the floor wrapping teddy in a long strip of material, making the workers laugh at his antics.

"He's learning to bandage his teddy," quipped one woman. "He's probably going to be a doctor like his father."

"I'm not too sure about that," Aunt Frances said as she swooped Harry up from the floor and unwound the cloth.

Just as they were ready to go out the door, Nell said, "Oh, just a minute. My thimble's not in my pocket. I must have left it at the table."

She hurried back to the table where she'd been working, but Edie could tell from her panicked expression that it wasn't there.

111

"Perhaps it's in your smock," Aunt Frances suggested.

Nell scurried to the back but came slowly out, shaking her head. By then, Mrs. Garland was there, asking what Nell was searching for.

"My beautiful silver thimble," Nell told her, unable to hide the sadness in her voice. "I can't find it anywhere."

Mrs. Garland had every worker stop what they were doing and search the room for the little thimble. Larry and Gloria even joined in the search. But after several minutes of going through all the pieces of cloth and through all the scraps on the floor, no thimble was found. Nell was near tears.

Edie put her arm about Nell's shoulders. "We'll find it, Nell. I'm just sure we will."

"*You* probably will find it," Sarah said as she sauntered closer to the two of them, out of earshot of the adults. "Because *you* probably stole it."

Edie waited for Nell to protest, but Nell was quiet, wrapped in her own grief.

Seeing she had an opening, Sarah added one more caustic remark. "Thievery is all you'd expect from a Hun anyway."

Edie went back to the Allertons' since she and Nell were to stay with the children for the afternoon. Dory had a big pot of vegetable stew steaming on the stove when they arrived. Aunt Frances invited Nell to eat lunch with them, but she said she'd better go tell her mama that she'd lost her precious thimble.

"I'll see you later," Edie said as Nell left, but Nell didn't answer.

By the time Aunt Esther arrived so she and Aunt Frances could leave for their meeting, Nell still hadn't returned.

"You go on," Edie insisted. "I'm sure she'll be here in a few minutes." She took Addy from Aunt Esther's arms and helped take off the little girl's fur-trimmed coat and matching hat and fur muff. Harry was taking a nap after his big adventure of shopping all morning. He'd probably sleep most of the afternoon, so Edie knew she'd do fine taking care of all four children by herself. Dory had left for her afternoon off.

"Telephone if you need anything," Aunt Frances said as they went out the door.

When the mothers were gone, Edie suggested they go to the playroom and play a game of Chinese checkers. She was surprised that even Larry agreed to the game. Larry set the wooden board up on Gloria's tea table, and Gloria got out the colored marbles, divided them up, and placed them in the proper holes. Edie held Addy on her lap as she went through the motions of playing the game, but she couldn't concentrate. As much as she fought it, the sad look on Nell's face after she lost the thimble kept coming to her mind.

Edie argued back and forth with herself about Nell. Surely she wouldn't listen to Sarah's wicked accusations. Surely she wouldn't. And yet Nell did not counter what Sarah had said. Perhaps Nell didn't even hear Sarah's accusations since she was so upset over the thimble. But if Nell hadn't paid any attention to Sarah, where was she now? Why hadn't she come back over to help with the children? The anxious thoughts whirling about in Edie's brain were wearing her to a frazzle.

Larry kept beating the socks off the two girls. He was an expert player even when Edie was at her best.

"You two play the next game," Edie said, putting her green marbles back into the box. "And I'll go down and fix us all a snack. Addy, do you want to go with me or stay up here with Gloria and Larry?"

Addy pulled her wet finger from her mouth. "Stay," she said softly.

"Come here, Addy," Gloria said. "You can sit on my lap."

As Edie walked into the kitchen downstairs, she looked out the back window to see if Nell might be coming across the neighboring backyards. That's the way she usually came from her house. There was no Nell, but she did hear a commotion in Mr. Benecroft's chicken pen. She lifted the kitchen curtain so she could get a better look. She leaned across the cabinet and looked again. "Gracious!" she exclaimed. "That's Harry!"

Not thinking to grab a coat, she slammed out of the back door and ran across the expanse of backyard. By now the chickens were squawking, flapping their wings, and carrying on something fierce, raising a huge cloud of filthy chicken pen dust.

"Harry!" she cried. "Harry, you come out of there this instant." Oh, why hadn't she checked on him? She'd thought he was sleeping soundly in his own bed.

"Chickie, chickie," he called out merrily. "Harry pet the chickies."

Frantically Edie ran up to the pen, trying to figure out how in the world he got in, but she saw no openings. There was nothing to do but unlatch the gate and go inside that filthy, smelly pen and fetch him out. She shivered, both from the bitter wind and the thought of smelly chickens and chicken droppings everywhere.

"Harry, come here!" she commanded as she lifted the latch and pulled the gate toward her slightly. If he'd come over to her, she could grab him and not have to go inside.

"Edie, catch me," he said running to the other end of the pen and sending squawking chickens everywhere, dust and feathers flying.

"Harry, this is *not* a game," Edie said in her firmest voice. She stepped inside and closed the gate behind her. If a chicken came at her, she was sure she'd collapse into a dead faint. Only if it were midsummer could the smell have been any worse.

"Harry, come here, or I'll have to tell your mama on you. You're being a bad boy."

"Catch me, Edie, catch me," he repeated.

The first few steps she took, Edie tried to avoid the smelly droppings. But there were too many. Then she became angry. "Harry Edwin Allerton, you come to me this minute!" She went at him with a vengeance and again the terrified chickens flapped their wings and squawked as though she'd come after them with a hatchet.

Just then she heard a loud voice yelling, "You kids get out of my chicken pen. You got no business playing in there."

Edie knew that was the voice of Mr. Benecroft. And he was angry. When she reached Harry, she grabbed at him and lifted his lead-weight little body. As she did so, her left foot landed in a slippery pile of droppings and whooshed right out from under her, landing her flat on her back in the dirt.

Harry, who landed unhurt beside her, was giggling. "Do again, Edie. Do again," he squealed, while Edie struggled to catch her breath.

Again came Mr. Benecroft's voice. "I said for you kids to get out of that chicken pen!"

Edie struggled to her feet, grabbed tightly to Harry's hand, and fairly dragged him out of the pen. Mr. Benecroft was standing at the gate. In fact, several neighbors had come out to see what was going on.

"What do you think you're doing in there?" Mr. Benecroft demanded as he let them out through the gate. "Those poor hens won't lay for a week."

Edie was cold, dirty, and thoroughly humiliated. "Little Harry slipped outside without me knowing it," she said, trying to catch her breath.

"Well, see to it you keep a closer watch on him after this."

"Yes, sir. I plan to do just that." She pulled at Harry's hand. "Come on, Harry. Let's get you inside. You're filthy."

The neighbors, seeing it wasn't anything to get excited about, dispersed to go back inside out of the cold wind. All except one. Nell stood in the middle of the yard bundled in her warm forest-green coat.

"Oh, Nell, there you are." Edie was so glad to see her. "I could sure use your help about now."

But Nell wasn't smiling. "Mama asked me to come out to see what all the noise was about. But I see now." She turned to go, then said, "Perhaps Larry was right. Perhaps you're not a very good mother's helper." With that she walked slowly back to her house.

The awful spill Edie took in the dirty chicken pen didn't hurt nearly as much as the cold rebuff from her dear friend.

Carl arrived at the Allertons' before the two mothers returned. He found Edie dressed in one of Larry's shirts and a pair of his knickers. She was fighting back tears as she attempted to wash out her smelly soiled dress at the kitchen sink. When she told him what had happened, he agreed to ride his bicycle back to their house to bring her a clean dress. His quiet kindness made her cry even more.

She didn't tell Carl about Nell. Or about the lost thimble. Or about Sarah Whalen coming to the center. In fact, she told no one. No one at all. What good would it do?

At least she and Harry were both clean when Aunt Frances returned. She quickly told her aunt exactly what had happened. She almost hoped she would lose her job, because she never wanted to come back over here near Nell's house again.

She never wanted to return to the Red Cross Center, either. What she really wanted to do was go to her bedroom, close the door, and never come out for a million years.

CHAPTER 16

The Secret Message

Aunt Frances and Aunt Esther agreed they should never have left all four children with Edie until they were sure Nell was coming. Even Gloria explained that none of them had heard little Harry slip out of his bed and leave the house—and his bedroom was located right next to the playroom. Edie thought it was sweet of Gloria to come to her defense. Surprisingly enough, Larry said nothing against her, either. But none of it mattered anymore.

After that day, everything became stiff and awkward and uncomfortable. Edie knew Nell would never be helping at the Allertons again. Somehow she was able to make lame excuses to Aunt Frances about Nell. Whether or not Aunt Frances understood, she didn't know, but at least her aunt didn't press for further explanations. Aunt Frances said she understood that friends sometimes had little quarrels. How Edie wished that's all it were—a little quarrel.

On the following Monday morning, Edie wasn't surprised when there was no Nell waiting for her at the schoolyard gate. As she walked into her sixth-grade classroom, Edie knew she had to be the loneliest person on the face of the earth.

Now instead of looking forward to Saturdays, Edie dreaded them. She watched as Nell sat with Sarah and Lorraine at the center. In the afternoons, Aunt Esther arranged for another girl to watch Addy, which broke Edie's heart. But again, she forced herself to believe that it didn't matter. Nothing really mattered anymore.

Sometimes she found herself wondering about God's promise of being faithful. Was He truly faithful? Was He truly her fortress and her high tower? There were many days when it seemed as though God had turned a deaf ear to her.

Days at school dragged out in endless minutes and hours. From behind her came the constant whispers and note-passing between Nell and Sarah. At recess and at lunchtime, Edie stayed mostly to herself. Of course Carl was often alone on the playground as well, but she couldn't very well play games with an eighth-grade boy, even if he was her brother.

Other German children were being ignored as well, but it would have been worse for all of them if they ever tried to band together. They'd all learned it was better to remain quiet and stay out of the way.

Edie couldn't wait for each day to be over so she could get home. At first Mama had asked her if she was coming down with something and felt her forehead to see if she had a temperature. "It's nothing," Edie told her. "Nothing's wrong with me."

"I do believe," Mama had said, "the whole family's in the doldrums."

Papa talked to them one evening about having grateful hearts and reminded them to give thanks to God in spite of their problems.

Edie knew that Papa, too, was going through incredible struggles. Shortly after the presidential election in November, one of their union meetings had been broken in on by a hostile group. The vigilante-type mob turned mean, breaking windows, calling ugly names, and slamming furniture around until the union men were run off.

Papa didn't say much about it, but Carl saw the article in the next day's newspaper. It told in detail how the union group had been run off, but that no one had been hurt.

When they asked him about it, Papa said, "People fear what they do not know. Since they do not take the time to learn what we are all about, they prefer instead to fight us." Smoothing his mustache, he added, "We shall find a better place to meet. The warehouse was too easy for them to locate."

In past years, Thanksgiving and Christmas had been Edie's favorite times of the year. This year Thanksgiving came and went almost without her noticing. She tried hard to do what Papa said and maintain a thankful heart, but it was so hard.

The week following Thanksgiving, a letter came from Truman. He described the bitter cold on the Western Front and the effect it had on the soldiers.

These men have been fighting the elements for so long, most have only dim memories of reclining in a soft chair and warming their feet before a toasty fire. Or scooting up to a table and eating good clean nutritious food.

As if the vermin and rats and the sickness that dwell in the trenches aren't enough, now the bone-chilling cold has come to multiply their misery. We see wounded men with frostbitten fingers, feet, and noses.

My heart goes out to these chaps who week after week hold the front and hold the Kaiser at bay. Oh if only we had the help of American troops.

Ever since Truman had gone away, the Schmidt family had written him a letter every week, each of them putting in a page of their own personal thoughts. At first it had been fun to think of things to share and then post their letter all the way across the ocean to France. But now Edie felt she had nothing to say.

Mama instructed them to be encouraging and cheerful when they wrote. "He sees enough of sadness and suffering," she said.

But it was as though Edie's cheerful "bank" was bankrupt.

While at Aunt Frances's house, Edie started scanning issues of *Life* magazine in an attempt to find something cheerful to write to Truman about. Perhaps a joke or a cartoon. When she did, she came across an illustration of a gigantic ugly brute with a glassy stare, a spiked helmet, and a bloody knife in his hand. Beneath his thunderous stride, tiny civilians were being crushed and destroyed. The caption read, *Germany, the Bully of Europe*. Below the picture the text read:

We ought to be sorry for the Germans. As we see them today they are a pathetic people. Germany has set up to be the bully of Europe. . . . And bullies are always stupid. . . . In his present stage of development, the German is the fat man of Europe whom nobody loves.

Edie threw down the magazine as though it were scalding. She made no more attempts to search through magazines. When it was time for the family letter to be sent to Truman, Edie told them she had nothing to add.

Lydia just looked at her. "But you always send a note to Truman," she protested. "He'll be so disappointed."

"Maybe I'll have something next time," Edie answered. She knew she was being small-minded and selfish, and it made the sad feelings inside her seem even more wretched.

Edie could remember when she and Lydia used to talk about things. All kinds of things. Edie had halfway thought that Lydia would talk with her about what had happened with Nell and then help her to sort out her feelings. But she never did. Lydia was too busy thinking about Truman.

She kept all his letters in a pale green box with ribbons and flowers on top—a box that stationery had come in. Sometimes she opened the lid and took the letters out and touched them reverently. Sometimes she would read through them. Edie wondered if Lydia was afraid something terrible might happen to Truman.

The first big snowstorm of the winter hit just before Christmas, blanketing the city in deep drifts of the white stuff.

Mama had spent hours each evening after work baking and preparing good food for the holiday. As usual they were all scheduled to gather at the Allertons'. But on Christmas Eve, yet another blizzard blew through. When they woke up, Papa and Mama decided they wouldn't even try to get to the Allertons' for dinner.

"We'll have our Christmas right here," Papa declared. That suited Edie just fine.

Because of the money she'd earned being a mother's

helper, Edie had been able to purchase Christmas gifts this year. She was proud of that fact. Mama taught each of her children how to budget money. Some of her money Edie gave to God, some she gave to the household fund, and some she saved. Her frugal savings had allowed her to purchase the gifts. They were small, but they were special.

The family exchanged their gifts in their own comfortable parlor, and then Edie, Lydia, and Mama set to preparing dinner while Papa and the boys attempted to shovel a path from the house to the street—and from the house to Carl's shed.

The day felt cozy and safe. After a big dinner, Edie snuggled up with her beloved Frosty and worked on her tatting, then read her new book that Lydia had given her. She didn't care if the snow ever melted again.

Of course she knew that was more of her silly thinking. If the snow stayed, then the trolleys couldn't run, the milkman and grocery drays couldn't get through, and Mama and Papa couldn't get to work. But for the moment she could enjoy the seclusion of the house and the safety of her family about her, and she pretended that it might last forever.

The Christmas snowstorm was the beginning of many such storms that winter, and the later storms weren't nearly as much fun. It was as though the entire city spent the winter digging out—and then digging out again. Many mornings Tim arose very early with Carl to help him with his big paper route since he was unable to ride his bicycle.

"Just like old times," Tim joked as he bundled up against the fierce north winds. Tim had thrown papers along with Carl before he began working at the engineering company.

If Edie had dreaded going to school before, she dreaded it even more now that the temperatures hovered below zero. Tromping through wet thick snow made the walk to school both uncomfortable and difficult. The only good part was that Carl's bicycle remained in the shed while the snow was deep. He walked by her side every day through the worst of the winter or walked just ahead of her to break a path through the deep snow.

Their neighbor Mrs. Bierschwale was ill quite a bit that winter. Uncle Richard must have visited at least half a dozen times. Edie took soup to her as often as she could get over there. Mrs. Bierschwale's husband, Bruno, was not a very kind man, and Mrs. Bierschwale was growing more crotchety with each passing day, which didn't make it easy to be in her presence.

Uncle Richard encouraged Edie to continue helping. "If we were in her shoes, we might very well be that crotchety and more," he said. Edie could almost understand what he meant.

On the first day of February, Tim and Carl returned from their route saying there was bad news in the paper. As the boys were removing their heavy wraps, Lydia read the article aloud. It said that Germany had openly declared that they intended to forcibly prevent any U.S. ship—or that of any other nation—from reaching England. They proposed to use "unrestricted use of the weapons."

Edie knew that meant that all merchant marine ships like the one Devlin Swearingen worked on would be in extreme danger.

Immediately after the announcement, President Wilson broke off all diplomatic ties with Germany. This meant that Count Johann von Bernstorff, the German ambassador to Washington, had to leave the country, and along with him went all the German consuls and their families.

Papa shook his head as Carl pointed out to him the photograph on the front page of the newspaper. It showed 149 Germans boarding a Danish ship to sail from New York back to Germany.

"It's getting closer and closer," Papa said softly. And none of them had to ask what he meant.

By the time St. Valentine's Day arrived, Edie was quite weary of snow and cold. She knew she wouldn't receive very many valentines anyway, and she didn't want to go to school that day. But of course she had to.

She and Frosty had become inseparable friends during the dreary days of winter—almost like Harry and his teddy. Holding Frosty close and feeling his soft contented purring made Edie remember the previous spring when things had been so good in her life. Thinking about the spelling bee was her favorite memory. How she had stepped up to receive her award, wearing her special yellow dress. How proud everyone had been of her; how they all fussed over her. But that was before Truman had gone away, before Devlin had left, and before she'd lost her very best friend.

One Saturday, Uncle Erik surprised the Schmidts by renting a cutter from the livery and coming by with the Allertons to take them for a ride. Laughter and singing blended in with the happy sounds of sleigh bells as the high-stepping horses pulled them all around the city. It was the first time Edie had had a good laugh in ever so long. How kind and thoughtful of Uncle Erik to think of such a thing—and to have included them. After the ride, they all ended up at Uncle Richard and Aunt Frances's house for hot chocolate and popcorn.

It'd been weeks since they'd all been together. The hard winter had restricted even the most simple of travel plans. Edie had missed all her cousins a great deal. But being at Aunt Frances's house also brought back all the memories of her good times with Nell. Edie felt as though her heart were breaking.

On Tuesday morning, February 26, Carl came in red-faced and

breathless from his route. Most of the walks were clear, so he'd ridden his bicycle once again. As he burst into the kitchen, he was waving the newspaper. "Look at this! Just look at this!"

He held up the paper so they could see the headlines: *Secret Message Decoded: Germany Plots Alliance with Mexico!*

Papa was just pulling on his coat to leave for work, but he took the paper from Carl's hand and sat back down at the table. He began to read aloud about the document that had been intercepted and decoded by British naval intelligence. The message had been sent by Alfred Zimmermann, an undersecretary at the Ministry of Foreign Affairs in Germany. The message promised Mexico that if they formed an alliance with Germany, Germany would give to them the states of New Mexico, Arizona, and Texas.

Mama sat down heavily in the nearest chair, her eyes wide with disbelief. "They would promise to give parts of our nation to Mexico? As though they'd already entered into war with us and won? What audacity! How dare they?"

"Who would have thought," Tim put in, "that the Kaiser would ever be that aggressive?"

"No one," Papa answered. "No one would have thought it." He stood up and grabbed his lunch bucket. Kissing Mama on her cheek, he added, "There is no doubt now that war is inevitable. Mr. Wilson has done all he can to maintain the peace, but this is too much. And," he said as he went out the door, "when Kaiser Wilhelm II takes on the Americans, he will have met his match."

CHAPTER 17

Missing in Action

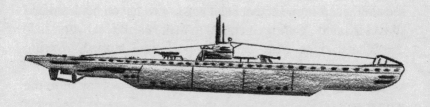

The day Edie saw the first purple crocus that March, she was going out to Carl's shed to tell him supper was ready. The abundance of melting snow had turned every bit of ground in the city into a sloppy muddy mess. In some places there were still piles of dirty snow that had not yet fully melted. As she stepped off the back stoop, she wasn't looking for flowers. She was diligently trying to avoid the ever-present mud puddles. That's why she nearly stepped on the tiny beauty. When she realized what it was, she stopped with her foot in midair and nearly tumbled over.

"Oh, look at you," she whispered when she'd caught her balance. "Just look at you coming up through the muck to say hello." She knelt down to touch the tiny petals. Now that she was closer to the ground, she saw several more crocuses pushing their brave green sprouts up and out. But none were in bloom except this brave one that she'd nearly crushed.

She drew in a deep breath. The air was still sharp and cold. New life. The purple crocus was a sign of new life. Almost like a little note from God, telling her that things that sometimes seem dead may not be dead at all.

"Little Edie," came a voice from the next yard. Mrs. Bierschwale was beginning work in her garden. One would have thought last winter that the older woman wouldn't live to see another spring. But there she was, straw hat on her head and shovel in hand. "Spring, it comes to make us all feel better. Ja?"

"That's right, Mrs. Bierschwale," Edie replied. "Spring certainly makes us all feel better."

"A good girl you are to feed this old lady as I lay ill in the winter months."

A thank-you from Mrs. Bierschwale? How refreshing that was. "I was more than pleased to help, Mrs. Bierschwale," Edie assured her neighbor. "More than pleased."

She hurried on out to Carl's shed and knocked at the door. No one dared open his door without knocking because sometimes he was developing film, and if light came in, the photos would be ruined.

When he opened the door, a wall of smelly chemical fumes came pouring out. "Phew," Edie said, waving her hand in front of her nose. "I don't see how you stand that awful smell."

"I have chemicals in my veins," Carl said, smiling. "Supper's ready, I presume?"

"It is."

"Good. I'm famished."

"As always."

One could hardly call Carl's darkroom a shed anymore. He'd worked steadily to reinforce it, insulate it, and to fix it up on the inside. Mama often said that if he added another room, he would probably live out there.

"When you come outside, watch your step," Edie warned him.

"The mud doesn't bother me, Sis," he quipped.

"No, I mean the crocuses. They're up."

Carl came out and closed the door, looking where she was pointing. "Well, I'll be. Maybe there will be a spring after all. I declare, I wasn't sure there for a while."

That evening as the family was eating a quiet supper together, the telephone rang.

Mama rose to answer it.

"I hope it's not another prank call," Tim mumbled through a mouthful of stewed chicken. "You'd think they could come up with a more original idea than telephoning and hanging up all the time."

"I prefer that over a rock through the window," came Lydia's wry retort.

Their telephone hung on the wall in the kitchen, and every time someone talked on it during mealtime, Papa had to scoot his chair over to make room. When Mama picked up the receiver, she said, "Oh, hello, Frances. We've just begun supper. . ." She stopped speaking in midsentence, and her face went white.

The room grew deathly still.

"I see," she answered. "When?" She nodded and said, "All right, I'll put her on." Covering the receiver with her hand, she turned to Edie. "Your aunt has something to tell you."

Edie felt her heart throbbing in her throat. She knew it was not good news. She took the receiver from Mama's hand. "Hello, Aunt Frances."

"Edie, I wanted you to know the Swearingens just received a telegram telling them that Devlin's ship was torpedoed somewhere in the North Sea."

Edie's chest tightened. "And Devlin?"

"Missing." There was a quiet pause. "I knew you would want to know."

"How is. . .everyone?" Strange. She couldn't even bring herself to say Nell's name.

"They're taking it very hard. I took food over just a while ago. Several neighbors were there, but Mrs. Swearingen couldn't even talk. Nell was upstairs in her room."

Edie nodded even though Aunt Frances couldn't see her. "We'll pray for them tonight."

"I knew you would."

When Edie replaced the receiver, she realized she had gripped Papa's shoulder without even knowing it. Poor Nell. Poor, poor Nell.

Papa reached up to gently pat her hand. "It's Devlin?"

"His ship was torpedoed. The Swearingens just received the telegram. Devlin's missing."

Lydia covered her face with her hands. Tim slapped his hand on the table making the water glasses jiggle. "How much longer will they be able to get away with this senseless murder?"

"Not much longer, I feel," Papa said softly.

"But haven't we taken enough?" Carl wanted to know.

"Our leaders know best," Mama said. But she didn't sound fully convinced.

"I'm not so sure anymore." Tim pushed his plate back with his dinner half-finished.

"No one seems to be hungry," Mama said. "Let's clean the kitchen and gather in the parlor to pray for the Swearingens."

As Edie helped wash the dishes, her heart was in agony for

Nell. Everything inside of her wanted to run to her friend to comfort and console her. But Nell had made it very clear she wanted nothing to do with Edie. Especially after the silver thimble came up missing. Edie's hands were tied. There was nothing she could do.

That night as they gathered for prayer, Papa put on his gold-rimmed reading glasses, turned directly to Psalm 18, and began to read:

> *The Lord is my rock, and my fortress, and my deliverer;*
> *My God, my strength, in whom I will trust;*
> *My buckler, and the horn of my salvation,*
> *and my high tower.*

"We will pray for God to be the fortress and deliverer in this hour of need for the Swearingen family," Papa said, looking around at each one of them. "These next verses are for Devlin." Smoothing the thin pages of the family Bible, he continued:

> *I will call upon the Lord, who is worthy to be praised:*
> *So shall I be saved from mine enemies.*
> *The sorrows of death compassed me,*
> *And the floods of ungodly men made me afraid.*
> *In my distress I called upon the Lord, and cried unto*
> *my God. . .*
> *My cry came before him, even unto his ears.*

Papa prayed for Devlin's life to be spared and that the young man would call upon the Lord and be saved from the enemy.

The next day, Nell was absent from school. Mrs. Corbitt

announced to the class about the telegram the Swearingen family had received. "Following our Scripture reading, we will remember Janelle and her family in our morning prayers," she said, taking the Bible down from the shelf.

From behind her, Edie heard Sarah whisper, "I bet Nell would be comforted more if someone hadn't stolen her silver thimble."

Edie acted as though she hadn't heard.

Mrs. Corbitt glanced in their direction and scowled, then went back to her reading.

The second day, Nell returned to school, but her eyes were swollen and red as though she hadn't stopped crying since the news came. Edie so wanted to remind Nell about the promises from Psalm 18, but she kept her distance and said nothing.

That evening Lydia asked Edie if she had gone to Nell since the news came. Edie shook her head, half-ashamed. "I can't. She doesn't want to see me."

"Are you sure?" Lydia asked. "It may be different now."

The two were getting ready for bed. Edie felt almost relieved that after all this time, she could finally talk about Nell to Lydia.

"It's no different," Edie countered. "Nell is friends with Sarah Whalen now. She doesn't look at me or talk to me."

Lydia sat down on the side of the bed. "Oh, Edie, I'm so sorry. I didn't know the rift was that deep."

"Deeper than the Grand Canyon," Edie said. She'd seen pictures of the Grand Canyon in the stereoscope pictures at Aunt Frances's house.

"But God can step across the Grand Canyon," Lydia said softly. "It's barely a finger-span for Him."

Edie thought about that for a minute. She supposed Lydia was right. "What should I do?"

"If you don't feel comfortable going to her, a letter might work. You can put a lot of love into a letter."

Edie's eyes went to the green box on the bureau. "Is that what you do?"

Lydia blushed. Edie had never seen her sister blush. "Unfair question," she quipped. "We're talking about you and Nell. How does a letter sound? Safe?"

Edie nodded. "I think I can write a letter."

"Good," Lydia said. "God can use the letter to span the Grand Canyon."

But writing a letter was easier said than done. Edie must have started a dozen times, and each time she ended up crumpling and tossing another sheet of paper into the trash basket in her bedroom. Nothing she wrote sounded right.

On March 9, President Wilson surprised the nation by announcing that all merchant marine ships would be armed with guns and gunners. The action was to be undertaken immediately. But before it could be put into effect, three unarmed American ships were sunk by U-boats. These were empty ships returning to the United States. They carried no contraband, munitions, or military supplies.

Papa said that Americans were now more than just hot under the collar. "Fighting mad they are now," he said.

Edie wondered if Truman had been right all along. If their nation did nothing to stop Germany, soon the Kaiser would rule the entire world. Perhaps there really were things in this world worth fighting and dying for.

CHAPTER 18

Good News!

Edie couldn't imagine what Nell must be going through, never knowing whether Devlin was dead or alive. She was unable to fathom that kind of agony.

Lydia continued to encourage Edie to write a letter to Nell. "You can do it," she'd say. "Just write until you get all the feelings dumped out on the page. If you don't give up, you'll finally be able to say what you truly mean."

At long last after many attempts, Edie finally put together a letter that spilled out the feelings from deep in her heart. She explained how much she loved Nell and how she valued their friendship. She thanked Nell for having been such a good friend through past months and thanked her for all the good times they'd had together. She expressed sorrow about Devlin and reminded Nell of the prayers of the Schmidt family. Then Edie stated that she couldn't help it that she'd been born into a German family with a German name any more than Nell could help being a Swearingen. She closed by writing:

> All of our family rejoiced to learn that President Wilson is arming the ships of the merchant marines. We are very much in favor of any and all actions that would work to stop the killing that is happening because of Kaiser Wilhelm.

Then she signed it with all her love. When she read it aloud to Lydia, her older sister smiled and nodded. "Mail it," she said.

The best part about spring was that Edie was once again a mother's helper at Aunt Frances's house. Gloria, who was now seven, said she was old enough to help. Between the two of them, Edie and Gloria convinced Aunt Esther and Aunt Frances to allow them to take care of both Harry and Addy. Edie could see right away that having Gloria's cooperation would make the arrangement much easier.

Addy was growing cuter and more outgoing. Her finger came out of her mouth long enough for her to say a few words. And Harry seemed to be about ready to give up teddy. The tattered old bear was carried around less often.

It was the last Saturday in March. The little ones were napping, and Gloria was playing dolls in the playroom. Who knew where Larry was? He'd received a bicycle for Christmas, and now he was all over the neighborhood. Edie decided to step out on the back porch and soak up the sunshine.

As she did, she saw teddy sitting on one of the wicker chairs. She picked him up as she walked by. She smiled to think that Harry was actually taking a nap without the stuffed toy. Perhaps he would go to first grade without the teddy bear after all.

Sitting down on the steps, Edie stretched out her legs and scratched at the woolen underwear beneath her long stockings. Just a couple more weeks and the underwear could be packed away. Edie could hardly wait.

Just then, she heard a voice. Startled, she looked up to see someone running across the backyards, heading pell-mell toward her. It was Nell!

"Edie!" she yelled, waving a paper in her hand. "Edie! Look! Look what I have!"

Edie jumped to her feet as Nell practically bowled her over, grabbing onto her and shaking her, laughing and crying all at the same time. "It's Devlin. He's alive! He's well!"

"Oh, Nell." Edie grasped her old friend and held her tight. "I'm so happy for you. So very happy."

"He's in Scotland. He was picked up by a fishing trawler near Aberdeen."

"Come here." She guided Nell to the porch steps. "Tell me all about it."

"Oh, Edie. Wait till you hear. It was the German boy."

"German boy?"

"Don't you remember? Wilmott Achleitner, the boy on-board his ship."

"What about him?"

"He saved Devlin's life."

Edie gasped. "Gracious."

"Just listen to this." Nell read from the pages in her hand.

There I was out on the open seas—choppy seas at that—treading water for all I was worth. It was the only thing out there that I could see. I didn't know if anyone else survived the explosion.

Oh little pint-pot, I don't know how you happened to think to send me Psalm 18 awhile back, but the words of that psalm kept ringing in my head all the time I was thrashing around out there. That and the song you mentioned, "A Mighty Fortress Is Our God." Over and over I kept thinking: A helper he amid the flood. . . *And I was definitely in a flood of sorts. Strange, don't you think?*

Nell looked at Edie and smiled. "Remember when you suggested I share that verse with him? Well, I did just what you said."

Edie was in a daze. She sat there hugging teddy in her arms as Nell read on:

This part is even more strange. As though out of nowhere, there was Wilmott. Just like an angel coming out of the mist. He was paddling toward me. He'd somehow managed to grab onto a piece of splintered wood and it was helping him to keep his head above the water.

He wanted to share his little lifeboat with me. So I shared my Scripture and my song with him. He said, "I know that whole song." So he sang every verse. Then he sang every verse in German. What do you think about that? Sounds ludicrous I know, but

*that's what sustained us throughout the long, cold,
dark night in the sea before a fishing trawler picked
us up the next morning.*

Nell was laughing and crying all at the same time. "Your hymn, Edie. The one you suggested that I share with him in a letter."

Edie squeezed teddy more tightly as her tears spilled over and trickled down her cheeks. Who would have believed this?

"Now listen to this part," Nell said, wiping her own cheeks with the back of her hand.

*People are still people, little Sis. Never forget
that. Never judge them by their name or nationality.
We may be fighting a force of evil that is coming out
of Germany, but that doesn't mean every German is a
bad person!*

"Oh, Edie," Nell said, catching her breath between sobs. "I'm so sorry for turning my back on you and for treating you badly. I've been so cruel and thoughtless. I thought when you didn't stand up to Sarah that that meant she was right in what she was saying.

"I know that's silly," Nell continued, "but that's what I thought. And after we learned Devlin was missing and I didn't hear from you, I thought sure you didn't care anymore."

Nell pulled a hankie from her pocket to swipe at her runny nose. "But your letter helped me to understand."

"I didn't know what to do," Edie admitted. "I thought if I ignored the problems, they would go away. But I see now that doesn't work."

"No more than ignoring Germany's attacks on our ships

is making the war go away."

Edie nodded. "You're exactly right." As she talked, she was kneading the soft bear in her hands. Suddenly her fingers detected something small and hard. She squeezed it again. "Nell, look here! Look what's inside of Harry's teddy bear."

Carefully she put her fingers into the hole in the back, into the soft stuffing, deep down into the center of the teddy's tummy. Now she could feel the hard metal. In a moment the beautiful silver thimble was lying in the palm of her hand.

"My thimble!" Nell squealed. "You found my thimble!"

Laughter intermingled with tears spilled out into the warm spring afternoon.

"Harry probably picked up my thimble that day at the center and stuck it inside his teddy," Nell said.

"That's exactly what he did," Edie agreed. "The little dickens."

"I never really thought that you took it," Nell said. "Not really."

"Thank you for that," Edie said.

"What a glorious day this is!" Nell jumped to her feet and began to twirl around the yard in circles. "Devlin's alive, and my silver thimble's been found!" she chanted in singsong fashion. Then she turned and ran back to Edie, grabbing her friend and hugging her tight. "And I have my best friend back!"

CHAPTER 19

War!

On April 1, 1917, President Wilson addressed a joint session of Congress and requested that they declare war against Germany. Although many people still protested war and longed for peace, that hope was a mere illusion. On Friday April 6, the war resolution was approved by Congress. America had at long last been catapulted into the war.

On that same day, Americans everywhere cheered as government agents seized ninety-four Germans ships lying at anchor in New York Harbor. Somehow it seemed like true justice, because they were some of Germany's finest freighters, tankers, merchant, and passenger ships.

The Schmidt family watched the events closely as Carl brought the paper to them first thing every morning. Later they learned that hundreds of German nationals were also rounded up. Suspicion against those of German descent was more pronounced than ever.

"Our lives will be totally changed now," Papa told them. "Not in small ways as they have these past months, but totally changed."

"How do you mean, Papa?" Tim asked.

"We have little military might to speak of. Our navy is dismal. It will take an entire reordering of our factories to prepare for war, let alone calling for men to volunteer to train to fight."

"Are you also referring to the way those of us with German names will be treated now that we are fully at war?" Carl wanted to know.

Papa nodded. "I believe bad feelings will escalate." But Papa was quick to add, "Never forget that our God is faithful."

"He's our fortress and our high tower," Edie added.

"Ja," Papa agreed. "A strong fortress He is."

Within a couple weeks, a letter arrived from Truman Vaught. "I'm coming home!" he proclaimed in large letters at the top of the page.

> *For all these months I've been longing for a*
> *chance to really help these fellows. Now, I have it.*
> *I'll be home as soon as I can to join Uncle Sam's*
> *Army. I'm looking forward to spending time with you*
> *and to sit down with you in your cozy, friendly*
> *kitchen and eat a home-cooked meal again.*

When I once more step onto the shores of France, I'll have a gun on my shoulder and a grenade in my hand. Then we'll see who is mightier in this war!

Edie tried to interpret her sister's expression as the letter was read. It was impossible to do so. Of course Lydia would be ever so grateful to see Truman, but then she would have to say good-bye to him all over again. Edie wondered how a person could endure that much grief.

When she talked to Nell again, she learned that Devlin, too, was coming home to join the army. Soon hundreds of young men would be marching off to war. Papa was right, things were quickly changing.

Though the days ahead seemed terribly frightening and totally unpredictable, Edie felt as though she'd already won a small war in her life. In spite of the thunder of distant guns across the ocean, she was surrounded by her big, loving family, and God had reunited her with her dearest friend, Nell.

God truly was faithful. He truly was a mighty fortress.

There's More!

The American Adventure continues with *The Great War.* America has entered the Great War, and daily life has changed. Carl struggles to raise a Victory Garden in their backyard while Edie tries to fix meatless meals and bake bread using less flour. But some changes are scary. Students are required to burn German books at school, and Carl and Edie continue to be persecuted because they have a German last name.

Then one night Papa doesn't come home from work. Finally the phone rings. Papa has been arrested. He is charged with adding ground glass to the flour at the mill where he works. Will anyone believe he is innocent?

You're in for the ultimate
American Adventure!

Collect all 48 books!